"Give me a gun." M̶a̶r̶y̶ ̶G̶r̶a̶c̶e̶ ̶h̶e̶l̶d̶ ̶o̶u̶t̶ a hand.

At Ned's lifted brow, she added, "I know how to shoot."

"I just bet you do, Miss Mary Grace Ramsey. Do you plan to shoot me the first chance you get?" He didn't really think she was there to kill him, but he threw out the question to gauge her reaction.

Her mouth dropped open and Ned wanted to believe she was innocent in all of this, but he'd learned a long time ago that an innocent face could hide a host of danger.

"You're a very rude man, Ned."

His lips curled upward at the corners. It was an odd sensation. One he hadn't felt in a long time. But he stilled when Krieger released a low, dark growl.

Ned sprang into action. He scooped Mary Grace into his arms as a bright orange detonation took place at the front of the structure and his cabin shook under the force.

He had a sinking feeling in his gut that this whole mess wasn't going to end well.

Liz Shoaf resides in North Carolina on a beautiful fifty-acre farm. She loves writing and adores dog training, and her husband is very tolerant about the amount of time she invests in both her avid interests. Liz also enjoys spending time with family, jogging and singing in the choir at church whenever possible. To find out more about Liz, you can visit and contact her through her website, www.lizshoaf.com, or email her at phelpsliz1@gmail.com.

Books by Liz Shoaf

Love Inspired Suspense

Betrayed Birthright
Identity: Classified
Holiday Mountain Conspiracy

HOLIDAY MOUNTAIN CONSPIRACY

LIZ SHOAF

HARLEQUIN LOVE INSPIRED® SUSPENSE

 LOVE INSPIRED BOOKS

Recycling programs
for this product may
not exist in your area.

ISBN-13: 978-1-335-23247-2

Holiday Mountain Conspiracy

Copyright © 2019 by Liz Phelps

www.Harlequin.com

Printed in U.S.A.

For the love of money is the root of all evil: which
while some coveted after, they have erred from the faith,
and pierced themselves through with many sorrows.
−1 Timothy 6:10

This one is dedicated to both of my wonderful sisters, Donna Wright and Sherri Stout. You're beautiful, inside and out, and I'm so blessed God chose you to be my sisters here on earth. Growing up was such fun with the two of you. You bossed me around, but you also protected and loved me like no one else ever could. That still holds true today. I love you with all my heart.

And a BIG thank-you to my editor, Dina Davis, who always catches my mistakes. What would I do without you? I don't want to find out. :) And to her boss, Tina, who has final approval of all books. There's a host of people at Harlequin who work on a book from beginning to end. I don't know all your names, but I want to thank you for the hard work you do to make the finished book possible.

ONE

Mary Grace Ramsey breathed out a puff of frigid air as she slogged through the deep, freezing snow. *Treacherous* didn't even begin to describe this mountain located in Jackson Hole, Wyoming. She prayed she'd be able to find the person she was searching for—a mysterious and elusive man known as Mountain Man. Her thoughts came to a screeching halt when a loud muffled sound resonated from down the mountain behind her. Snow flurries swirled in the air as she slowly turned around, trying to make as little noise as possible. She winced when the snow crunched beneath her hiking boots. In the hushed quiet of the forest, the breaking ice under her feet sounded like a cannon shot.

"Tink, did you hear that?" she whispered.

A tuft of white fur, followed by a pink nose, popped out of the nylon dog carrier she had strapped to her chest. Tinker Bell sniffed the air before ducking back inside her cozy quarters.

"Some help you are," Mary Grace grumbled affectionately, but she didn't blame her dog. Mary Grace's own nose felt like an icicle and her toes were freezing to the point of pain. She owned decent outerwear, but nothing in her closet would have kept her warm in this brutal weather.

She strained to hear something, anything, but the vast forest remained quiet. She turned and slowly moved upward, praying earnestly that she was headed in the right direction. Huge pine trees heavy-laden with snow-covered limbs towered above her like skeletons in the waning daylight. Shivering inside her ski jacket, she prayed she'd find Mountain Man soon—and what kind of a name was that?—because there was a real possibility of her and Tink freezing to death if she didn't locate the cabin Sheriff Hoyt had described.

It was her stepbrother's fault that she was in this untenable situation, hiking into the wilderness in the dead of winter. The day after she found the note Bobby had left her, telling her she was in danger and needed to find the Jackson Hole Mountain Man, she'd sensed someone following her. On the way home from a press briefing at the White House that evening, a car tried to run her off the road. It was no accident. She was afraid to contact the police because of the warning in Bobby's note, advising her not to trust anyone inside the Beltway.

She'd tried repeatedly to get in touch with her brother, to no avail. It was as if he'd fallen off the face of the earth. His boss at Langley would only say that Bobby had requested a leave of absence, but as she well knew, the CIA was in the business of keeping secrets. And as a White House press correspondent for FBC, Future Broadcasting Company, it was her job to uncover them.

Mary Grace stopped, took a deep breath and scanned the area. Visibility had dwindled even more. Nothing but snow, ice and trees surrounded her. A deep, scary-looking ravine dropped off to her left. There was no cabin in sight and she was chilled to the bone. What if once she found the cabin, Mountain Man wasn't even there?

With no signal for GPS, she pulled her compass out of her pocket and checked it once again. According to what the sheriff had said, she should be close to her destination.

Tinker Bell popped her head out of her carrier and barked, and a split second later, Mary Grace heard the loud report of a rifle shot echo on the mountain. Before she even had a chance to run, fire ripped through her right side and she was thrown toward the deep ravine.

Her eyes closed as she floated soundlessly through the air. It was an ethereal experience. She wondered if this was what heaven would feel like, all light and buoyant. Pain ricocheted through her body when she forcefully hit the side of the mountain and was once again thrown into the air. Time seemed to slow before she finally landed on her back in a deep snowbank. After she caught her breath, her dire situation came flooding back. She was alive, but the killer was still out there. Slowly, she wiggled her arms and legs to see if anything was broken. Everything was stiff, but no bones screamed in pain. Her dog! She'd only bounced off the mountain once and she prayed her precious baby was okay.

"Tink! Tink? Answer me. Are you okay?"

When she tried to push herself up, pain seared her side. She gently dropped back down and ran her hands across her chest. She breathed a sigh of relief when she identified the dog carrier still attached to her body. She dug inside the nylon bag and grabbed Tinker Bell. Her side burned like fire when she lifted the Chihuahua toward her face, but relief overwhelmed her when Tink snorted and growled.

"You're okay," she breathed and hugged the dog close to her chest. But for how long, was the question. She touched the clothes covering her right side and groaned when her hand came back covered in blood. The reality of their situation was grim.

She and Tink were stranded on a freezing mountain in the middle of winter. She had been shot. No one knew where they were besides the sheriff. She had no way to call him, and there was a killer out there who wanted her dead. The worst thing was that she didn't even know why. *What has my brother gotten me into?*

She tried to push herself up again, but almost passed out from the pain. She fell back into the snow as darkness blanketed the area. At least she and Tink were no longer easy targets with the night shadows and the huge snowbank somewhat hiding them. Maybe the shooter would leave, thinking she was dead.

Time passed, but instead of feeling cold, a circulating warmth enveloped her body. In the recess of her mind, she knew this wasn't a good sign, but her eyelids grew heavy and she didn't seem to care. She wondered if she would soon meet her Maker. Her grandmother's face swam across her mind. Who would take care of the proud, independent older woman if Mary Grace died? Certainly not her own mother and stepfather with their gambling addiction. She didn't even know where they were most of the time.

As she lay there, halfway between sleep and wakefulness, she thought of her latest romantic fiasco. She'd dumped John Stiles after three months of dating. She couldn't seem to make a relationship work, or rather she didn't have a desire to after growing up in the dysfunctional household of her youth.

Now she'd never get married and have a family of her own. She and Tink would die on this beast of a mountain in the middle of nowhere.

A noise pierced the deep slumber she was descending into. It sounded like Tink barking. But maybe it was a dream. Or maybe the killer had found them, after all.

Nolan Eli Duncan, known to the world only as Ned, woke abruptly from a short nap in a cold sweat, fragments of the familiar, recurring nightmare lingering in his mind. The stench of blood and betrayal filled his senses. A soft bleep, bleep sound in the small cabin swept away the remaining splinters of his past, and with minimal movement and sound, he slipped out of bed and pulled on his holey faded jeans. He ignored the sting of the cold wooden floor against his bare feet.

Opening a drawer in the kitchen, he pressed a hidden button. A well-oiled portion of the counter automatically lifted and his laptop and security cameras rose to counter height.

Krieger, his long-coated, old-fashioned giant of a German shepherd, padded softly to his side.

"Security breach. Probably a bear," he grumbled, but his eyes narrowed when he brought up one of several security cameras and went to live feed. A large person dressed in winter fatigues wearing a ski mask came into view. "Or maybe," he whispered, satisfaction flowing through him, "the person who betrayed me and Finn has finally come calling."

He tensed when the guy wearing the fatigues lifted a high-powered rifle to his shoulder and scanned the woods through the scope. "He's tracking something… or someone, on my mountain."

Krieger went on full alert, ears pricked, ready to move on command. Ned's breath caught when one of the roving security cameras slowly swept past a huge snowbank. Was that blood on the snow? It was getting dark so he switched to night vision. He typed a command on his computer and operated the camera manually. There! He stopped the motion and zoomed in. There were large splatters of blood on the snow. He followed the trail, but the snowbank blocked his view.

Motionless, he stared at the blood, then glanced at the other camera, showing the guy in fatigues creeping closer to the ravine. He turned on the camera's sound.

When a sharp bark pierced his ears, he glanced back at the monitor showing the snowbank. His brows lifted when the smallest rat of a dog he'd ever seen popped onto the top of the snowbank. At least he thought it was a dog. It was solid white and had tattered limp Christmas bows attached to its ears. And if he wasn't mistaken, the dog was also wearing a Christmas sweater. He shook his head at that bit of nonsense and focused on the matter at hand. That meant a person was stranded in the snowbank and his assumption was that the guy in fatigues was an unfriendly.

"Krieger, protect the civilian and dog. I'm right behind you."

With barely a whisper, his dog flew out of the hidden dog door and took off down the mountain. Ned donned his inner and outerwear quickly and opened a concealed panel on the cabin wall. It was all legal, but he'd compiled a small arsenal, waiting for his enemies to come after him.

He slung a long-range rifle across his chest, stuffed a handgun into his pocket and shoved a large knife inside the holster strapped to his calf. He grabbed a first-aid kit and was out the door.

The action wasn't far from his cabin. He didn't know if that was accidental, or if someone was searching for him, but he'd find out soon enough. His long legs and steady tread covered the quarter-mile distance with ease. He'd been living on this mountain off and on for several years and knew every nook and cranny. He'd spent a fortune on security. He had enemies, dangerous enemies.

But that wasn't the only reason he'd holed up on his mountain for months. He had somewhat become a recluse after the betrayal, much to his family's dismay, and he no longer liked, or trusted, most people after everything he'd been exposed to during his clandestine missions. Everyone had an agenda and many would do anything to get what they wanted. He'd be content living by himself on his mountain after he rooted out the worm who had betrayed him and Finn.

He picked up his pace as the thrill of the hunt coursed through him. After all this time, he hoped the carefully laid bread crumbs he'd left several months ago for the betrayer to follow had finally led the person to his mountain for a showdown. Although in reality, he knew the odds were low that the person who originally set the trap would do his, or her, own dirty work.

When he closed in on the coordinates, he slipped his fingers under the cross-body strap and lifted his rifle into his hands. It was second nature and the weapon felt like an extension of his arms. He hid behind a large tree and listened. The soft crunch of boots came from a one o'clock position. He moved, following the sound. Experience had taught him how to walk in the snow without making any noise.

Ned caught sight of the person several hundred yards ahead. He speculated, based on size, that it was a man, but in his line of work, it paid not to make assumptions. He wanted to subdue the person so he could question them, but someone was injured—maybe dying—in that snowbank, and he couldn't take any chances.

At least he had that much humanity left in him. Lifting his rifle—armed with a silencer, he scoped the guy. Even though Finn had lived through their nightmare, a gory vision of Ned's best friend and comrade going down from a gunshot wound flooded his mind. For a split second, he aimed the gun at the man's head, then lowered the barrel and pulled the trigger.

The bullet soundlessly puffed the snow up at the man's feet. The guy's head snapped around and Ned moved from his cover into an open position, his rifle pointed straight ahead. The man's eyes narrowed from behind the slits in the ski mask. Through the scope of the rifle, Ned snapped a mental picture of those blazing violet-colored eyes. He'd recognize them if they met again unless the man was wearing contacts. The guy lifted his own weapon and moved backward, keeping his gun trained on Ned. No question, the guy was a professional. Was he after Ned, or the person lying in the snowbank?

Krieger popped his head over the top of the ravine. Ned gritted his teeth as he allowed the man to get away and followed his dog. He'd probably just blown two months of a carefully planned trap because of the person who had fallen into the ravine.

He scooted down the steep hill and approached slowly. Krieger stood on alert at a caved-in portion of snow, but gave no indication of danger. As Ned stepped closer, the tiny rat dog he'd seen on the security camera at the cabin popped out from behind the freshly disturbed snow. The small dog barked ferociously at Krieger and Ned's fierce, highly trained giant of a German shepherd went into a down position and whined. Ned did a double take. His dog never whined. The little mutt growled when Ned brushed away a mound of snow and discovered what had caused him to miss a possible golden opportunity to get a lead on his betrayer.

He huffed out a frustrated breath. It figured it was a woman. A beautiful woman whose eyelids fluttered open after he jerked off a glove and touched her neck with his cold fingers to see if she had a pulse. In past missions, he'd met women who looked soft and vulnerable, but turned out to be killers in disguise.

Her golden eyes widened in fear seconds before they flooded with determination and fury. "Go ahead and kill me if that's your plan, but you better not lay a hand on my dog."

The woman passed out using the last reserve of her strength to protect the rat. An unexpected ping resonated near the region of Ned's heart, but he ignored it. He pulled his glove back on and started gathering the woman in his arms, but the tiny dog ran toward its owner and buried itself inside the pouch of some kind of dog carrier, similar to a backpack, strapped to her front.

Ned picked her up as if she weighed nothing and started climbing the steep hill. He didn't know how long she'd lain in the snow, but he hoped she wouldn't die. That could complicate matters. He ignored the small flame of hope that had sprung inside his heart when she'd opened her eyes and fiercely tried to protect the dog. Maybe she loved the animal, but there was a reason she'd shown up on his mountain, and it couldn't be good. Everyone had an agenda and he didn't trust anyone outside his family and Finn. Humanity, in his eyes, was a lost cause.

TWO

Mary Grace slowly awoke from that wonderful, murky place somewhere between sleep and wakefulness and winced as she stretched. Her limbs were stiff and her right side burned like fire. She vaguely remembered being on the mountain… The mountain! She'd taken a bullet and had fallen into a ravine.

She shot upright in bed, sucked in a startled breath at the pain in her side and popped her eyes open. She screamed when a large creature that looked way too much like a wolf opened his mouth and big sharp, gleaming white teeth came toward her. She threw up her arms to protect her face, but instead of razor-sharp blades piercing her arm, she felt a rough tongue gliding against her skin.

The ache in her side left her gasping for air and it was in that helpless, vulnerable state that she noticed a bear of a man sitting in a chair facing her, a roaring fire burning in the stone fireplace behind him.

Was this the elusive Mountain Man she'd been trying to locate, or was he the person who shot her on the mountain? Or were they one and the same? Bobby trusted Mountain Man, but she'd rely on her own gut when she figured out who he was. Not that she was in any condition to defend herself or get away if it came down to it.

Her heart racing, she quickly scanned her surroundings and wasn't at all happy with what she discovered. There were two doors in the small cabin. One appeared to be the front door and the other smaller door probably led to a bathroom.

She took a deep breath and locked a steady gaze on the man. She did her best to achieve what Gram Ramsey always advised in that strong, independent, proud Georgian tone of hers, *Always use proper manners, but don't ever let 'em see you sweat. Look like you're strong and know what you're about, even if you're quivering inside like Jell-O.*

She prayed she'd make her grandmother proud and lifted her chin. "Where's my dog?"

The man just sat there and kept staring at her like a knot on a log. The keen observation she was known for in her chosen profession as a journalist went active. The man appeared to be a throwback from mountaineer times. He was huge, really huge, with dark bushy hair that brushed the collar of his plaid shirt. An unkempt beard covered most of his face. Unblinking, razor-sharp green eyes stared back at her. He wore holey ancient jeans. She noticed a heavy fleece jacket hanging on a coat rack placed next to the front door.

He was large, like in a mountain-man-horror-film type of big, which directly opposed the odd tendril of attraction she felt when those green eyes flickered with a small degree of warmth. Her body ached, her side felt like an inferno and testiness quickly replaced any lingering terror.

She ignored her unreliable feelings where men were concerned and blurted out, "I said, where's my dog?" There! That came out sounding firm and in control. At least she hoped it did.

A sound came from a lower wall beside the kitchen counter and a portion of the wall lifted inward, allowing Tinker Bell inside the cabin. Mary Grace's fingers tightened on the plaid blanket thrown over her and she was really wishing she'd brought the gun safely tucked away in her Arlington town house with her.

Her eyes widened when Tink approached the bed and the big wolf dog moved to the side so her baby could hop up beside her. She held Tinker Bell to her chest, closed her eyes and said a quick prayer, asking the good Lord to keep her safe, then took a deep fortifying breath and lifted her lids. She subdued the nervous laughter bubbling up inside her as she wondered if the man had even blinked while her eyes were closed. He hadn't moved a muscle since she'd woken up.

"Who sent you?" His words sounded gruff and rusty, as if he didn't talk much.

"Are you Mountain Man?" She inwardly rolled her eyes. Thus far, they had exchanged a few two- and three-word sentences. Her colleagues would find her situation amusing because she was widely known as a shark disguised as a soft-spoken Southern woman. She had a talent for squeezing every tiny bit of information out of the politicians on Capitol Hill without their even realizing it. She attributed her success to her Southern upbringing, and she didn't think those particular attributes would work on this big, solid mountain man, but she'd give it her best shot.

She dug deep and dredged up a sweet, soft smile. He couldn't have been the person trying to kill her on the mountain. He'd had plenty of opportunity to do away with her and hide her body while she was unconscious. Her fake smile wavered as she felt the bindings on her side pull and she wondered if this crazy mountain man had patched her up, but she kept her smile in place.

"Why don't we start over. My name is Mary Grace Ramsey, and no one sent me. Well, that's actually not true. My brother did send me, but that's a long story and I need to find a man everyone refers to as Mountain Man. The sheriff in Jackson Hole said people around here call him Ned. He's supposed to help me. But then I got lost on the mountain and someone started shooting—"

"Stop!"

His bellowed word sounded pained and he rubbed his forehead.

"Do you have a headache? Maybe you should take some aspirin. I've always found that—"

"Stop!" he bellowed once again. "Just be quiet for a moment."

Her chattering was already working. This wasn't a simple mountain man. Under duress, his short verbal gruffness had revealed a sophisticated speech with an underlying Scottish brogue.

He closed his eyes for a minute, then blinked them back open. "Are you for real?"

Mary Grace rubbed Tink's head. Time to make good use of her famous interview skills. "I'm not sure how to answer that question, but if you're Ned, then we definitely have several things to discuss, and sooner would be better, considering someone shot me earlier."

Seeing the stunned look on his face, she gave him a big, warm Georgian smile.

He attempted to smile back, but it looked more like a feral grin, throwing her game back in her face. "Who's your brother?"

He had picked out the key part of her chattering, which shouted of intelligence. She'd have to tread carefully around this man.

"Well, technically, he's my stepbrother, but I refer to him as my real brother because we're very close."

His chair slid back as he stood and walked to the side of her bed. Her fingers tightened on Tinker Bell as he towered over her. He was even larger than she had originally thought, but she forced her hands to relax.

"Your brother's name?"

It really made her mad when her hands shook. "Bobby Lancaster."

His eyes narrowed, and his large hands fisted at his sides. Deep, abiding fear sliced through Mary Grace, but she gallantly lifted her chin and glared at him.

He leaned over her and Tink and his long beard tickled her chin, he was so close. "Where is he?" he breathed in an ominous tone.

Fury filled Ned when Bobby Lancaster's name rolled off her lips. It didn't help his disposition that he found the irritating woman beautiful, either. She had light brown hair with sun-kissed streaks winding through the strands, and those golden eyes of hers were enough to bring a man to his knees. He imagined her soft-spoken Southern accent encouraged people, both men and women, to spill all their well-kept secrets.

He refused to fall into her trap.

"Where's Bobby?" Anger made his words sound harsh. He almost regretted his question when she scooted away from him, toward the wall that the bed was pushed against, but he didn't move.

The rat growled, but Ned ignored it until his own dog pushed his way between Ned and the bed. He was stunned. Krieger was protecting the woman and her dog. He growled at Krieger and his dog growled back. He couldn't believe this little slip of a woman had turned his trusted companion against him.

Ned knew his mother would have been appalled at the way he was treating Mary Grace Ramsey, and his dog might have decided to trust her, but that little ping he'd felt in his heart right after she spoke for the first time and defended her rat dog went still. A dark wall of mistrust replaced any minute tender feelings he had allowed himself to feel.

His gut clenched when her lower lip quivered, but he felt justified in his wariness when she pasted on another warm smile.

"I take it you know my brother, and that must mean you're Mountain Man, or rather Ned. I'm so glad I found you. You wouldn't believe what I've been through—"

"Stop!"

Ned backed away from the woman and winced at the expression of relief on her face. Maybe he did need an aspirin. He grabbed the wooden chair from in front of the fireplace, flipped it backward close to the side of the bed and straddled it. He nudged Krieger out of the way, leaned forward and folded his arms across the back of the chair.

"Let's start over. Yes, I'm Ned. I want to know exactly why you're on my mountain and I would highly advise you to tell the truth."

She scrunched up her pert little nose. "My gram would have something to say about your manners and hospitality."

He leaned back in his chair, crossed his arms over his chest and waited. It took less than two seconds. The woman could probably talk the hair off a dog.

"Fine. You know my name. Bobby is my brother, and two days ago I found a note from him that someone had slipped into my tote bag. It said he's in big trouble, but that he's innocent and for me not to trust anyone inside the Beltway or I might get myself killed. That's where I live, you know. Well, not actually inside the Beltway. I have a sweet little town house just outside the city in Arlington—"

Ned couldn't help himself, he released a low growl and she quickly got back on track.

"Sorry, anyway, he told me to contact you, that you're a big part of whatever is going on and that you could protect me. I'm really glad I found you, because besides getting shot here, I'm pretty sure someone tried to run me down in the city. I was afraid to call the police because of Bobby's warning, so here I am."

"Where's Bobby?" Ned now wanted to wring her stepbrother's neck for several reasons. He'd planned to personally interview Bobby if his carefully laid plan to draw the bad guys to his mountain didn't work out, and he'd also wondered if Bobby had been coerced to do what Ned had proof he'd done. Either way, Bobby was involved in the mission that left Ned's best friend in a wheelchair for life and now he'd placed his own sister in danger.

Unless Bobby had sent her to Ned's mountain to finish the job someone had botched in England—to rid the world of Ned and Finn. Another startling question begged to be answered—how had she found him? Only a handful of people knew where he'd holed up.

She picked at a thread on the plaid blanket. "I, um, don't know where Bobby is." She lifted her head and started gabbing again. "And that's the honest truth. I tried calling him and even called his boss at Langley. They said he was on leave. I'm really worried. Bobby and I are pretty close. You see, he was only eight years old when my mama decided to marry his daddy—"

She stopped talking when Ned raised a hand in the air.

"I'm not interested in your life story." He leaned forward again. "How did you find me?"

He could almost see the wheels turning behind those sharp golden eyes. She might act like a silly Southern debutante, but Ned had learned long ago how to cut through a ton of garbage and grab the nugget hidden inside. His gut screamed that she was smart as a whip, and he seldom read people wrong. The question was whether she was telling the truth or planned to slit his throat the first chance she got.

She pulled the thread completely out of the plaid blanket and tossed it to the floor. The fact that she didn't have a ready answer told him she was carefully weighing her words.

"The note Bobby slipped into my bag said I was in serious danger and that I'd be safe with *Mountain*

Man, who was currently residing in Jackson Hole. The sheriff gave me directions to this mountain, and I was afraid Tink and I were going to freeze to death before I found you."

She rubbed a hand across the quilt and stared at the unique coloring. "Is this some kind of a special design? Kind of like the tartan colors they use in Scotland?" She glanced around the cabin again. "And speaking of colors, you don't have any Christmas decorations."

Based on the hideous Christmas sweaters the woman and her dog were wearing, Ned assumed she was a big fan of the holiday, but he made sure his expression revealed none of his hidden thoughts. He hadn't celebrated Christmas in a long time.

He studied her a moment longer and a facet of her personality settled in his gut. Her chatter and speech slowed down when she went on a fishing expedition, and she was trying to find out more about him, hence the question about the quilt. She must have picked up on his Scottish accent, which proved her power of observation was keen, but he didn't have time to play games. The man he had allowed to get away was still on his mountain because the perimeter alerts would have gone off if he'd left.

He had to determine if the intruder was after him or Miss Ramsey. Speaking of which…

"Are you married?"

Her head jerked up and her light brown eyebrows scrunched together.

"There's a killer out there and you want to know if I'm married?" Her voice raised several octaves higher.

He didn't see anything wrong with the question. It always paid to know whom you were dealing with. He denied the tiny niggle in his chest telling him he wanted to know for personal reasons. That was preposterous. This was about finding Bobby Lancaster and dealing with the people who wanted him and Finn dead, and that was it.

He stared at her without blinking.

"Fine, I'm not married, nor have I ever been."

He couldn't stop the next question that shot from his mouth. "Boyfriend?"

She sniffed. She actually sniffed, reminding him of a little old lady.

"Not that it's any of your business, but I don't have a boyfriend. At least I don't have one at the moment."

The tightness in his chest eased and he had no idea why. Her incessant chattering must have scrambled his brain.

"Forget the chitchat. We have a big problem on our hands. I need all the information you can give me. The man who tried to kill you is still on the mountain, and I need to track him down, but first you have to tell me everything."

Those golden eyes narrowed, reminding him of a mother panther getting ready to strike while defending her young.

"Do you think that's why Bobby's in hiding, because someone is trying to kill him, too?"

"You're sticking to what you've told me? You know nothing more?"

Exasperation filled her voice. "I've told you everything. Bobby somehow got me that note, telling me to leave DC and find you. Someone tried to run me down in Washington, and then they tried to kill me on this atrocious mountain."

Ned's mind worked furiously. He tried to think of a way to rid himself of Mary Grace Ramsey, but her brother had pulled her into this mess, and Ned's best opportunity of finding the possible traitor was to keep Bobby's sister as close as possible. Whether major or minor, Bobby was part of what had happened to him and Finn. Whether by choice or not was another matter. Now that Mary Grace Ramsey was in the picture, his plan to lure those responsible to his mountain was trashed. Her brother had now become his only lead and he had to find him.

He rose from the chair, crossed the room and reached for his jacket.

"Where are you going?"

He didn't hear a speck of fear in her voice. It was more of a demand. He had to give her credit, the lady had guts.

He shoved his arms into the sleeves and strapped the high-powered rifle to his chest.

"I'm going hunting."

She winced as she threw her legs over the side of the small cot. "But you can't just leave me here. What if he comes back?" She held out a hand. "Give me a gun." At his lifted brow, she added, "I know how to shoot."

He didn't respond and she lifted her chin. "I'm from Georgia. I know how to handle a weapon."

"I just bet you do, Miss Mary Grace Ramsey. Do you know how to use a knife, too? Do you plan to slit my throat the first chance you get? Are you and your brother working together to get rid of me and Finn?" He didn't really think she was there to kill him, especially after she'd been shot trying to find him, but he threw out the question to gauge her reaction.

Her mouth dropped open and Ned wanted to believe she was innocent in all of this, but he'd learned a long time ago that an innocent face could hide a host of danger.

"You're a very rude man, Ned."

His lips curled upward at the corners. It was an odd sensation. One he hadn't felt in a long time.

He placed his hand on the latch to open the solid wooden door, but stilled when Krieger released a low dark growl. Ned sprang into action. "Krieger, to the cellar," he commanded. He was by Mary Grace's side within a few strides. He scooped her into his arms and ran to the back of the cabin.

"Wait," she screeched. "I don't know what's going on, but you have to get Tinker Bell, the dog carrier and my backpack."

Ned shifted Mary Grace to his left side, holding her like a football, wincing when she gasped in pain, and in one fell swoop he ran his arm through the straps of both packs on the floor, grabbed the dog by the scruff of the neck and kicked a lower panel on the back inside wall of the cabin. A portion of the wall lifted just as a huge explosion rocked the small structure.

Ned practically dove into the yawning darkness below as a bright orange detonation took place at the front of the structure and his cabin shook under the force. The woman was screaming and squirming in his arm and her rat dog bit his hand while he was trying his best to save them. He had a sinking feeling in his gut that this whole mess wasn't going to end well.

THREE

Throwing up became a real possibility for Mary Grace. She gritted her teeth against the pain in her side as Ned held her tight with one arm while running down a flight of stairs into total darkness. She couldn't believe someone had bombed the cabin. Was there more than one man following her on the mountain? She was used to reporting the news, not being part of it.

"Hang tight. We should be okay. The cabin is built with reinforced steel under the wood."

She couldn't respond. Air hissed through her teeth until he gently placed her on the floor. She took a deep breath as a lantern flickered to life. The light reflected on Ned's fierce, concerned expression and she took another quick breath to calm herself. A mass of emotions roiled through her. Fear and—she couldn't believe it under the circumstances—still that annoying attraction to the man currently hovering over her. It wasn't possible. She barely knew the guy and he had the manners of a warthog, but there it was, the tiniest little flutter in her heart. She ignored it.

Tink whimpered and Ned's big dog trundled over to

offer what Mary Grace assumed was comfort. It worked because Tinker Bell quit shivering and growled when the massive dog licked her on the face. The limp and tattered Christmas bows had disappeared and her sweet little dog looked like a wrung-out dishrag in her previously pristine doggy Christmas sweater.

Tentatively, Mary Grace reached out and laid a hand on the large animal next to her little one. "Sweet Krieger. Nice doggy." He allowed her to pet him. His fur was long and felt wiry to the touch.

"Mary Grace," Ned said in a soft tone, "I'm going to have to recon the area. I bandaged your wound before you woke up, but I need to check and see if it started bleeding again."

Mary Grace didn't want to talk about the explosion and the men who had just tried to decimate them. Not just yet. She needed a minute. "When we get through this, you'll have to tell me how you and Krieger met. He seems like a sweet dog, once you get to know him."

Ned kneeled in front of her and placed the lantern on the hard, cold dirt-packed floor.

"I was wrong about you."

Her hand stilled in Krieger's wiry, comforting fur. "What?"

"I thought you were tough, but here you are, wimping out on me at the first sign of trouble."

Her nostrils flared at the insult. "You don't know anything about me, so how dare you accuse me of being a wimp."

He grinned and she realized he had done the same thing to her that his dog had to Tinker Bell.

"I can check my own wound," she said, embarrassment threading through her words.

Mary Grace lost her train of thought when he smiled again, revealing a set of perfectly aligned, sparkling white teeth. The man definitely wasn't what he appeared to be and her reporter's curiosity was roused. Maybe she'd do a piece on him once they were out of this mess. He had a closet full of secrets and she could literally smell a story.

"I didn't know you were modest." He actually chuckled. "Don't worry, the bullet went straight through the fleshy part of your waist. Even though you bled a good bit, it's not a serious wound."

"Easy for you to say."

He stood and towered over her before reaching for something under the staircase. He came out with a pistol and handed it to her. "You said you knew how to use one of these."

She grasped the gun and looked it over. "SIG Sauer P38. Perfect."

He chuckled one more time before climbing the stairs. Over his shoulder, he issued a command. "Krieger, protect the woman and dog."

Before she could protest, he disappeared silently through the hidden doorway.

Her hand shook as she checked to make sure the gun was locked and loaded. She had done her best to hide her true emotions from Ned. She was not only terrified at the situation she found herself in, but worried sick about Bobby. As far as she knew, her brother was a simple computer analyst with the CIA. They had lured him in straight after school by offering to pay off his college loans if he'd work for them for five years. Mary Grace had advised him against it because she knew how naive Bobby was and how political the CIA had become. She offered to help him until he got established, but he was determined to make it on his own.

After rubbing a hand over her wound to make sure it wasn't bleeding, she picked up the lantern and held it high, checking out the cellar. It wasn't very large— about half the length of the cabin. Both the walls and floor were constructed with hard-packed dirt, but the interesting thing was the canned food and water stored on crude shelves built against the wall. Matches, several more lanterns and a first-aid kit were there if needed.

Settling her back against the wall, she kept the gun in her hand and her ears peeled for any sound coming from upstairs. Both Krieger and Tink snuggled beside her, and she decided to review the information she had so far. It helped to keep her calm and her mind from wondering whether Ned was okay out there on that freezing, fierce mountain with killers running loose.

She knew next to nothing about the man living on this mountain in the middle of nowhere. Was Ned his real name, and what was his last name? What did he do for a living? Her reporter's curiosity had been roused and she knew from experience that she wouldn't stop until she found out everything there was to know about the man.

In her mind's eye, she went over what she'd seen of the cabin, searching for clues. The place itself wasn't much to look at. Log walls. A tiny kitchen/living area. The bed she'd lain in was pushed against the wall and there was one door, besides the obvious front door, that probably led to the bathroom.

What struck her was the neatness of the place. It made her think of military precision. An old couch with a ratty afghan folded across the back sat in the middle of the living area. A coffee table squatted in front of the couch, but there were no side tables. No computers or TV anywhere. Mary Grace's eyes narrowed as she remembered seeing a large landscape painting hanging on the wall beside the bed. She had only glanced at it, but the quality seemed out of sync with the cabin, so she filed the information away. In the past, she'd broken stories wide open by taking note of the smallest details.

She shivered and both dogs snuggled closer. She knew she should do a better check on her wound, but she didn't want to lose the warmth of the animals.

Chewing her lower lip, she tried not to worry about Bobby, but she couldn't stop herself. He was the only family that counted outside of Gram Ramsey. She still prayed for her mother and stepfather, but had pretty much given up hope of them overcoming their gambling addiction. She smiled as she thought of her grandmother. The older woman was a spitfire and Mary Grace knew this time of year the old historic house would be traditionally festooned with Christmas decorations— a lot of them made by Mary Grace and Bobby when they were kids—and a huge live tree. Gram stood about five feet two inches in her stockings, but her strong will and absolute faith made her seem ten feet tall. She had withstood the tests of time with an elegance that Mary Grace could only aspire to.

A scratching noise upstairs jerked her out of her

musings. Krieger got to his feet and quietly stood at the foot of the stairs. Reacting quickly, Mary Grace clamped a hand over Tinker Bell's snout before the dog could bark. She held her breath and heard a shuffling noise that sounded like someone walking through the remains of the cabin. Whoever it was stopped at the top of the stairs.

She held Tink up to her face. "Shh. Don't bark. Please."

Slowly, she released her hand, and when she was sure her dog would stay quiet, she scrambled to her feet, ignoring the pain in her side, and crossed to stand beside Krieger. She willed her hands to stay steady as she lifted the gun and held it with both hands toward the small hidden door at the top of the stairs. It hadn't been long since Ned left, and it could be him returning, but what if it wasn't?

The panel started to open, and she tightened her grip on the gun, ready to stop the killer.

Standing from his crouch over the footprints he'd discovered circling around to the back of the cabin, Ned's head had snapped up and his body tensed when he heard a snowmobile coming toward the front. Sound carried differently in the mountains and there was no way of knowing how close it was. By the time he raced around the structure, someone had already entered the cabin.

His pulse pounded as he called on years of training and forced himself to relax. He slowly mounted the steps, then sidestepped the front door, which hung by the top two hinges.

"Uncle Ned?"

The tentative, fear-filled words froze the blood in his veins.

He'd warned his family to stay away from the cabin until he notified them, but his niece, Fran, was an intelligent, determined twenty-four-year-old woman currently working on her master's in advertising. What scared him was that his niece was on the mountain at the same time as the killer. He stared at her, standing in front of the open panel that led to the hidden basement. He didn't know if Mary Grace would realize Fran was friendly, but before he could control the situation, Krieger bounded out of the opening with the woman on his heels, the rat dog tucked under one arm and the gun in the opposite hand. He was relieved to see the weapon quickly lowered to her right side.

Fear stamped on her face, Fran glanced between the two of them, then dropped her gaze to the gun in Mary Grace's hand.

"Uncle Ned?"

"Aye, niece, I'm here. Everything's okay."

He opened his arms and Fran flew against his chest. She shivered for a few minutes, then pulled away. Propping her hands on slim hips, she attempted to show bravado, but Ned could see the fear lingering in her eyes.

"It looks like you've gotten yourself into a real mess this time." She slanted a questioning look toward Mary Grace. "Wait till I tell Mom and Grandfather."

Ned shook his head and went along with her stab at courage. "Ye and yer mother canna seem to stay out of my business. 'Tis embarrassing."

With a triumphant glint in her eyes, Mary Grace

scooted forward and he gently took the gun from her hand when she got close enough to get in his face.

"I knew you had a Scottish background. I just knew it."

She appeared very pleased with herself until Ned cut a sharp glance toward Fran, sending her a message to keep quiet about his private life.

Mary Grace took a step back, folded her arms across her chest and tapped her foot. "I saw that."

He ignored her astute observation and addressed his niece. "Sweetheart, I know you're a grown, independent woman, living at home while you work on getting your master's, but does your mother know you're here? You know she worries." Fran might be twenty-four years old, but she still managed that sweet, pleading look that always turned his heart to mush. He lifted a hand.

"Never mind. We have to get off this mountain. I'm pretty sure the guy who bombed the cabin is gone, but there's no way to be certain."

Both ladies tensed, and he could almost smell their fear return. He mentally shook his head. How, after meticulous planning and patiently waiting, had these two women ended up in his cabin at the exact moment his enemy had decided to attack? If it was indeed his enemy and not Mary Grace's. It was implausible, at least concerning Mary Grace. But she was connected to all of this through her brother.

He had to track down Bobby Lancaster and he needed Mary Grace to make that happen.

"Did you check your wound?" Her hesitation answered his question. "Do it now and do it fast. We're leaving in ten minutes." He turned to Fran as Mary

Grace flew back down the stairs to the basement. "Did you see anyone on your way up the mountain?"

Fran's eyes widened. "Y-you mean like the person who did this to your cabin?"

Ned nodded. "Didn't you hear the blast?" He felt bad about scaring her, but she needed to know the gravity of the situation.

"N-no. I couldn't hear anything above the noise of the snowmobile." She glanced toward the darkened stairwell. "Was she hurt in the blast?"

"Her name is Mary Grace Ramsey. I found her in a ravine with a gunshot wound well before the bomb was detonated." He rushed out an explanation when Fran's face paled. "She's fine. Just a flesh wound."

His niece lifted big blue eyes full of love that sent an arrow straight to his heart. "Uncle Ned, are you in trouble? I couldn't stand it if anything happened to you."

"Aw, come here, lassie." He folded her in his arms, then placed his hands on her shoulders and pulled her back, looking straight into her eyes. "Now havenae I always come back home in one piece?"

She grinned, and he was glad to see it. "Your accent always shows itself when you're emotional."

"Aye, that it does." He grinned and stepped back. "Now, let's get off this mountain."

Mary Grace cleared the top step. The dog carrier was strapped to the front of her body and she winced as she slid the straps of her backpack over her shoulders. "I'm all for that," she said, and gave him a look, practically daring him to mention her wound. "I'll be fine and I'm ready to leave. I left my car at the base of the mountain."

Ned led the way to the front door, but came to a grinding halt when he heard a sharp bark behind him and his niece squealed. "You have a dog! What a precious little thing."

Waiting for both women to come up behind him on the front porch, Ned scanned the frozen tundra surrounding them, but he didn't sense the presence of another human being. He'd checked a half-mile perimeter around the cabin and at the front of the structure found the remnants of a simple bomb. It had an attachment that appeared as if the device had been detonated remotely. Whoever tried to kill them had left the mountain. He felt it in his gut.

"Stay close."

He heard Mary Grace grumble to Fran behind him. "Your uncle is certainly a man of few words."

Fran whispered, "He wasn't always this way."

Ned sent her a sharp look over his shoulder and Fran zipped her lips. He pulled the shed door open and started checking his snowmobile.

Mary Grace sidled next to him. "What are you doing?"

"Making sure no one has tampered with my equipment."

Her eyes rounded and she didn't ask any more questions, which suited him just fine. He'd talked more since meeting her than he had in a long time.

"Fran, you'll take your snowmobile. I'll strap Krieger in behind you. Mary Grace can ride with me. I'll take the lead, but you stay close. I want to get you back to your mother safe and sound."

"But, Uncle Ned—"

He interrupted what he knew was coming. Fran and Sylvia were always at odds these days, and normally he would try to help, but now was not the time.

His voice was loving, but firm. "We'll talk later."

Everything checked out, so he fired up the snowmobile and motioned for Mary Grace to hop on. He didn't miss her wince of pain as she threw her leg over the seat.

"Hold on tight."

She placed her arms around his waist and Ned felt an unfamiliar warmth at her touch. He attributed it to the fact that he hadn't dated or even been around many women in the last few years. Ignoring the sensation, he pulled in front of the cabin. Fran was already seated on her snowmobile and ready to ride. She'd strapped Krieger in herself.

Ned took two helmets from the side of his snowmobile and handed one to Mary Grace. When they were both ready, he took off and Fran followed closely.

If he were still a praying man, he would have sent up a quick prayer for their safety, but he'd learned not to trust anyone but himself, and that included a God who allowed good people to get hurt.

It didn't take long to reach the bottom of the mountain, but fortune wasn't on his side. They pulled to a stop beside Mary Grace's car and there stood Sheriff Jack Hoyt, his arms crossed over his chest. Ned cut the engine and helped Mary Grace off the back of the sled. Fran was already off her snowmobile and came to stand beside Ned.

Ned nodded at the lawman. "Sheriff."

Sheriff Hoyt nodded back. "Ned."

He heard Mary Grace grumble. "What is it with this town? Do all the men speak in one-syllable words?"

Ned ignored her and watched the sheriff. He didn't have time for any delays or long explanations. He hoped the mountain and snow had muffled the blast enough that it hadn't been heard in Jackson Hole.

Hoyt's brows lifted as he nodded at Fran, then focused on Mary Grace. "Saw your vehicle on the side of the road and figured you'd decided to try to find Ned."

To her credit, Mary Grace pasted on a friendly smile and her explanation didn't leave any openings for questions. "I sure did, and I appreciate all your help."

Hoyt turned to Fran. "Didn't know you were familiar with Ned."

Taking her cue from Mary Grace, Fran grinned at the sheriff. "I've seen him around a few times."

Ned slowly released the breath he'd been holding. His family understood he didn't want anyone in Jackson Hole to know he was related to them for their own safety. One day his past might catch up with him.

Hoyt leveled a disbelieving look at the three of them, but cracked a grin when Mary Grace's dog stuck its head out of the pouch and barked. The sheriff moved close and rubbed its fluffy white head.

"Aw, what a cute dog. I have one of my own. Left him at the station today."

Hoyt stepped back and gave them all a hard look. "So everything is okay here?"

Ned's gut clenched when Mary Grace gave the sheriff a wide, welcoming grin.

"Absolutely," she said, "and I'm sorry for leaving my car on the side of the road. Ned's driveway was impassable, so I hiked to his cabin. Well, we'll just be on our way now. I'm sure you'd like to get back to the station where it's warm."

Hoyt gave them one last lingering look, nodded and folded his long frame into his patrol car.

Maybe living alone on his mountain hadn't been a good idea, because when Mary Grace gave that warm, gracious smile to the sheriff, Ned wanted to strangle the guy.

Maybe he'd been isolated for too long and it had affected his brain.

FOUR

Mary Grace hunched over the steering wheel in her rental car as she followed the two snowmobiles in front of her. Ned had said Fran lived several miles away.

She checked the heater to make sure it was on full blast. She'd never been so cold in her life. She'd take the sticky, sweet humidity in Georgia any day over these bone-chilling temperatures.

She couldn't imagine Ned living all alone on that isolated mountain. But maybe not completely alone. She now knew he had a sister and a niece. They evidently visited periodically. When she awoke that morning, she assumed he was all alone, because why in the world would anyone choose to live sequestered in complete isolation?

Tinker Bell growled when Krieger stuck his massive head between the bucket seats.

"It's okay, Tink. Krieger just wants to be friends."

Tink growled one more time for good measure and Krieger disappeared into the back seat. The dogs reminded Mary Grace of her and Ned. Uptown girl meets gruff mountain man. She chuckled at the comparison, but sobered when she remembered riding on the snowmobile with her arms wrapped around his waist. Something had stirred deep inside her. It was attraction and that was ridiculous. She didn't even know what his face looked like. It was almost completely covered by a beard that appeared as if it hadn't been groomed for months. Her grandmother would have been horrified by his appearance. About the one thing she was sure of so far was that the man calling himself Ned apparently loved his niece and, judging by his reaction, loathed Mary Grace's brother.

He was an enigma. She had to find out everything about Ned's connection to Bobby so she could protect her brother. She had no idea what was going on, but she'd find out. It was her gift—ferreting out secrets and information.

Outside of his negative reaction at the mention of her brother's name, the only thing Ned had actually said about Bobby was when he asked if she and her brother were working together to get rid of him and Finn.

Who was Finn and why would someone be trying to get rid of both men? But the most disturbing question was how her brother was involved in this situation. The people after Mary Grace and Bobby weren't playing games. Even though she finally felt warm, she shivered at the thought of the recent attempts on her life. She prayed Bobby would be safe until she could resolve this situation.

Her reporter's curiosity piqued once again when she made a right turn behind the snowmobiles onto a long driveway that appeared manicured, even beneath the snow. After making several soft turns, a large house loomed at the end of the driveway. A sizable fountain stood in the middle of the circular drive, complementing the wood and stone structure. She wouldn't classify it as a mansion, but it definitely came under the heading of mini mansion.

She cut the engine and flung open her car door. This was her best chance to find out more about Ned. There was no name on the mailbox and she needed information. She'd always had great rapport with other women. One mention of their cute kids or their pets or their boyfriends/husbands and they were usually off and running. Politicians would be the exception to that rule. She had to break out the big guns for those interviews.

She had one leg out of the car when Ned silently appeared and halted her momentum with a big bear claw on the door, stopping her from reaching her goal: to talk to his sister.

"You stay here. I'll be back."

His quiet but firm order really burned her. The terror she'd experienced on the mountain had melted away and she was more herself now.

She jutted her chin out. "Why should I?"

His expression didn't change, but she noted the twitch in his left eye, the only thing that remotely revealed what he was feeling.

"Because I'm the only one who can protect you while we look for your brother."

Like she was born yesterday. "For all I know, you want to kill Bobby. Why should I trust you?"

Her heart palpitated when he grinned for the second time since she'd met him, and her gut clenched. No, no, no, she absolutely refused to be attracted to this bear of a man. He hovered over her open door like a caveman.

He had to be at least six and a half feet tall. She considered herself of average height at five feet six inches, but he towered over her. He wasn't skin and bones, either. She briefly wondered how much muscle was hidden beneath those layers of clothes.

"Because your brother sent you to me."

Well, that took the wind out of her sails. He was right. Bobby had sent her to Ned. With little grace, she jerked her leg back inside the car and grabbed the door handle. It'd serve him right if his hand got caught in the door, but that wasn't to be. He showed his superior strength by holding on to the door until he was ready to release it. She gritted her teeth and pulled hard. He let go suddenly and the door slammed shut, rattling her hand.

Fuming, she crossed her arms over her chest and watched as Ned met Fran at the sidewalk and together they walked through the front door, firmly closing it behind them.

"Tink, I don't trust that man, not with Bobby's life on the line."

Tink barked and Mary Grace jerked when a big, rough tongue licked the side of her neck. She turned her head and looked at Ned's dog. "If only you could talk." The animal's eyes were full of intelligence and she remembered how Krieger had followed Ned's orders right before the explosion. She sat upright in her seat. Was Krieger military or police-trained?

As happened when she came across a vital piece of information while pursuing a story, her adrenaline took a sharp spike. She reached across the console and grabbed her backpack from the passenger floorboard of the car. Dropping it onto her lap, she dug through her belongings until her fingers wrapped around her cell phone. She lifted it triumphantly in the air.

"Ha! Got it." Tink barked her approval and Mary Grace held the smartphone close to her chest. "Now, if I can get a signal, I'll be in business."

She turned on the phone and fidgeted in her seat, willing the phone to power up fast. She wanted to do a quick search on Krieger before Ned came out of the house. Her heart beat faster when two bars appeared. Opening the search engine, she typed in Krieger—military dog and pressed the search tab. The blue line at the top had never taken so long, but when it finished, she grinned. There were several articles that popped up immediately.

The first one caught her attention and her nose actually twitched. She was in what she called her "reporter zone," a place where her gut told her she was on the right track.

It read: *Old-fashioned, giant German shepherd musters out with handler after six years of service in Army Special Forces.*

Mary Grace quickly skimmed the article, looking for a reference to the handler, but it never gave a name. She checked several other articles, but nothing. They did list all of Krieger's achievements and they were quite impressive. She glanced over her shoulder.

"I appreciate your service to our country, Krieger."

Tink growled again, but Mary Grace ignored her and scanned the house and grounds, searching for anything that would give her a clue she could follow to find out Ned's true identity. Then an idea popped into her head. She opened Google Maps on her smartphone and a map popped up. She got the address of his sister's house from there and was just following up on that when the driver's door whooshed open.

"Move over, I'll drive."

Mary Grace scooted over the console into the passenger seat and quickly sorted through all her options. She could probably, eventually, find Bobby on her own, and she was uncertain why Ned wanted to find her brother. Was it for information, or had Bobby inadvertently done something to anger this quiet, lethal mountain of a man? On the other hand, there were people trying to kill her and she wasn't quite ready to meet her Maker. Ned could protect her. She'd stay with him for the time being and try to figure out what was going on. If he would bother saying more than two words, she could make faster progress. She was a whiz at research.

"Fine, but you're going to have to start talking or I'll find Bobby on my own."

For a moment, Mary Grace had amused Ned. Through her eyes, he could almost see her brain rapidly processing her options, but then she smirked. She was up to something.

As he pulled out of the driveway, he glanced at her and considered her demand for answers. She was staring out the window and the rat dog—he really should call it by its name, but Tinker Bell just didn't feel right slipping past his lips—was glaring at him. The small dog and its name were enough to unman a guy. Concentrating on TB—that's what he'd call the animal—helped him to ignore the unwanted pull of attraction. Instead of answering her questions, it was time he asked a few of his own and got back to the task at hand.

"Do you have any idea where Bobby might be hiding?"

She turned her head and glared at him, much like her dog.

"Why do you want to find my brother? Bobby said you were a big part of *this*, whatever *this* is."

He stopped the car at the end of the driveway and turned toward her. Her jaw was set at a stubborn angle and her lips were pressed together. He had to give her something or she might bolt, and Mary Grace Ramsey was the only lead he had at the moment. His gut told him Bobby could lead him to the people who were after him and Finn.

All the evidence he had accumulated so far involved Bobby Lancaster, but the geeky young man just didn't fit the profile of a killer, which is why Ned had been trying to lure the bad guys to his mountain.

He'd soon find out where the CIA's computer wonder boy had holed up. At this point, he didn't care who he tipped off. Bobby had gone on the lam recently, and the ambush had happened six months ago, but it had taken Ned four months to get Finn settled, make sure he was okay and then lay his trap for their enemies. Prior to this, he'd stayed on his mountain between missions. No one in town knew when he slipped away and returned because of his hermit-type lifestyle, and he'd made sure no one knew he was related to his sister and niece because danger might follow him from current or previous missions. As far as the townspeople and anyone he worked with knew, he was all alone in the world.

Bobby must have been alerted by something, or found himself in a tight spot and took off. His gut told him that Bobby had to be involved because he'd fed Ned and Finn the bad intel that placed them in danger. Whether it was voluntary or involuntarily, well, that was yet to be determined.

"It's classified." She snorted, and he rushed to add, "Fine, I spent some time in the military a while back. You can trust me."

She didn't even respond to his admission of a small part of his past, instead she started typing on her phone.

"What are you doing?"

She lifted her head and gave him a challenging grin. "It's over two thousand miles to Georgia. You wanna drive or fly?"

He was onto her game. To fly, a person had to present identification. He grinned back and whipped out an encrypted satellite phone. He tapped in a number and held the phone close to his ear. There were two clicks, and he knew his contact was listening. "I need the private plane in Jackson Hole, pronto, headed to—" He looked at Mary Grace and almost laughed out loud at the stunned expression on her face.

"Waycross, Georgia," she answered through gritted teeth.

"Waycross," he repeated into the phone. "We'll be at the airport in thirty minutes. No paperwork."

He put his phone away and turned left out of his sister's driveway.

Mary Grace settled into her seat and kissed her dog on top of the head. He felt a mood shift in the car. It was almost as if he could sense her switching gears in that agile brain of hers. He liked the challenge of matching wits with her. He'd always appreciated beautiful women, but it was the smart ones who held his attention, and Mary Grace had proven to be very intelligent.

"Why Georgia?"

"That's where we grew up for the most part, at my grandmother's house." She turned toward him, as much as her seat belt would allow. "Unlike you, I have nothing to hide. Bobby and I were both born and raised in Georgia. My father passed away when I was twelve. My mom remarried quickly—way too soon for decency— and Bobby became my little brother. I was a little over thirteen and he was eight years old at the time. I helped take care of him."

She twisted back around and became interested in the passing scenery as she continued, "Bobby and I spent most of our youth at Gram Ramsey's house. We had what everyone now refers to as a dysfunctional family. Our parents were, and still are, pretty much gambling addicts. They traveled a lot and we stayed at my grandmother's house."

This time the chatter was laced with an undertone of hurt and regret and it made Ned even more curious about Mary Grace. But he clamped down on the sudden protective instinct that rose to the surface as she matter-of-factly discussed a childhood that had to have been fraught with heartache.

He empathized with her pain more than he wanted to and it was time to get the conversation back on track. He had to find Bobby.

"Why would Bobby go to Georgia? If his family lives there, that's the first place anyone would look for him."

Relief hit him full force when he glanced at her. The right side of her mouth kicked up and the challenge was back in her eyes.

"You ever been to a swamp, Mountain Man?"

He had fought the enemy plenty of times in a swamp, but decided to let her win this round. For some foolish reason—a reason he didn't examine too closely—he wanted to see the now-familiar smirk back on her face.

His hands relaxed on the steering wheel as he turned onto the road leading to the airport. "There's a first time for everything."

After waving his hand at the guy at the gate, he pulled onto the tarmac right up next to the plane.

Mary Grace gave him an incredulous look. "You can't just drive onto the tarmac without permission, and don't we need to go inside and see about the car return and go through security?"

He grabbed her hand, stopping her. "The car will be taken care of and we don't need to go through security. Stay close to me until we're on the plane."

She stared at him for a full minute, then pulled her hand away, her eyes narrowing. "Is this legal? Am I going to end up in jail?"

He couldn't help it, he grinned through his beard. "Everything is legal, and no, you won't end up in jail."

She stared at him a moment longer. "Who are you?" she asked, then grumbled, "Never mind. I'm sure it's classified."

She didn't sound as if she believed him, but after he called Krieger, she and TB did follow him onto the tarmac toward the plane. He stopped halfway there when the fine hair on his nape rose. Mary Grace ran into his back and he pulled her under his arm. Smart woman that she was, she didn't fight the maneuver.

"What is it?" she asked, her voice muffled under his heavy fleece jacket.

"Stay close to me and run when I say go."

The instinctual warning system that had saved his life on more than one occasion was screaming a red-hot alert. He took two more steps, moving them closer to the plane before he gave a quiet command. "Go. Now."

Mary Grace shot out from under his arm, clamored up the steps and barely got through the door before Ned heard a ping on the steps leading into the plane. He took a giant leap forward and slipped into the plane before the sniper could take another shot. Unfortunately, he still didn't know whom they were shooting at—him or Mary Grace. The bullet could have been meant for either one of them. But the one thing he was sure of was that they needed to get out of there before the sniper found a way to ground them…and finish the job.

FIVE

Mary Grace's heart thundered ominously inside her chest as she cleared the open door of the plane. Someone had shot at her. Again! A dangerous mixture of fear, adrenaline and fury had her whirling around as soon as she got safely away from the door. She released an undignified oomph when she hit a rock-solid wall of muscle. Ned hissed out a frustrated breath as she slammed into his chest, then caught her by the arms when she bounced off.

Tinker Bell yelped inside the dog carrier strapped to Mary Grace. Horrified she might have injured her dog, she lifted her from the pouch and held her high. Krieger whimpered at Mary Grace's feet and the tiny dog responded with a half-felt snarl.

Assured her dog was okay, Mary Grace took a relieved breath and placed her on the floor of the plane, then allowed both the dog carrier and the backpack to slide off her shoulders onto the carpet. Jerking her gaze toward Ned, she looked up, way up, and snarled herself. She felt as tiny as her dog standing in front of the six-and-a-half-foot giant and she wasn't used to feeling intimidated.

Still shaken up from the close call, her words came out sharper than intended. "Don't you think we better get out of here before whoever is out there shoots the fuselage?"

He nodded curtly and disappeared into the cockpit.

Mary Grace put on a brave act for Ned, but the seriousness of their situation shook her to the core. She prayed that Bobby was someplace safe and that no one was trying to harm him.

The loading stair door closed and Mary Grace took a deep calming breath and glanced at her surroundings for the first time. Her breath caught in her throat when she took in the luxurious interior of the plane. Or maybe it was a private jet.

Her eyes narrowed at the oversize leather seats placed strategically in groupings throughout the plane. Each area had an oblong table in the middle, and if she wasn't mistaken… Tromping down the center aisle, she lightly ran a finger over the top of a highly polished table. Yep, it was definitely teak wood and very expensive.

She walked to the back of the plane, jerked open a door and slowly entered a huge bedroom with a king-size bed sitting smack-dab in the middle. She stalked around and discovered a super fancy bathroom. Gold faucets gleamed from a sink surrounded by a green marble countertop. Teak cabinets completed the look. She slid open the shower door and discovered gold fixtures matching the ones in the sink.

Mary Grace mentally slapped her forehead. She was a seasoned reporter and she had made assumptions about Ned that she shouldn't have. Everything she'd learned pointed at him being in the CIA, or the military, in some form or fashion, but good ole Uncle Sam didn't provide rides as nice as this one.

She had a ton of questions, but she was mesmerized by the gold fixtures in the shower, wondering if they were made of real gold. Leaning over, unable to help herself, she took her fingernail and started scratching the faucet to see if it was real.

"You're a real snoop, you know that? And you shouldn't be leaning over like that with the wound in your side."

The low, gruff voice startled her so bad she jerked up from her bent position and heard an oomph from behind her as the back of her head slammed into his chest. If he weren't so tall, she could have clipped him on the chin, and wouldn't that have been a shame.

She whirled around. "Who owns this jet, and shouldn't we be taking off? Have there been any more shots from the gunman? We were fortunate the first shot only hit the steps."

He ignored her questions, turned on his heel and whispered out of the room. It was uncanny how such a large man could move so quietly, which demanded even more answers.

She followed him but came to a dead stop when he disappeared into the cockpit again. Surely he wasn't going to fly the plane. Was he?

She stuck her head through the small door and there he sat in the pilot's seat, flipping a bunch of switches.

"Um, where's the pilot? Are you planning on flying this plane?"

"Yes."

Mary Grace shivered. She was getting more nervous by the second. "Don't you have to file a flight plan?"

He did look up at that question and his white teeth sparkled from beneath the messy beard. "A flight plan has already been filed, but we're actually landing at a small, relatively unknown airfield in Georgia, near Waycross."

"What about when we don't land at the planned destination?"

"There'll be records showing we landed where we were supposed to." He refocused on the controls and waved toward the copilot's chair. "Take a seat. We'll be leaving soon."

Slowly sliding into the chair, Mary Grace closed her eyes in frustration. Bobby had gotten her into this mess, and now she was worried about her own safety, as well as her brother's. Just *who* was Ned, and how was he mixed up with Bobby?

There were too many unanswered questions, and she wasn't sure she could trust Ned.

"I see you agree with me."

The question snapped her out of her unsettling thoughts. She blinked her eyes open and stared at Ned as the plane rolled down the runway.

"Agree about what?"

He grinned, but kept his eyes straight ahead as the wheels of the jet left the ground.

"Trust no one."

Ned's own words reverberated in his mind. He didn't trust anyone, and that included the woman perched in the seat beside him. Oh, he might be attracted to the feisty little scrapper from Georgia, but he would never act on it. He preferred a simple life these days, free of emotional entanglements and betrayals.

But that didn't mean he wasn't concerned for her welfare.

"How's your wound?"

She slid him a sideways glance and he didn't miss the suspicion shining out of her eyes. Well, welcome to his world.

"It's fine. Like you said, it's a flesh wound. It'll be okay in a couple of days."

Ned rolled his shoulders to get the kinks out. Even working for the CIA, before he'd taken a leave of absence, he'd lived in something vaguely resembling peace until he decided to bring the enemy to his mountain, but then Mary Grace had shown up and turned his life upside down.

"Why don't you make use of the shower." He flashed her a grin. "And to relieve that curious mind of yours, the fixtures aren't solid gold, but they are gold-plated."

Her stubborn chin jutted out. "I'm not going anywhere until you tell me who owns this plane, and it better not be a two-bit dictator from some obscure little country."

"You don't have to worry, the plane is aboveboard, legally owned by an upstanding citizen of the United States." It was time he got some answers of his own. "We haven't had time to discuss you. Are you risking a job with your disappearing act?"

She turned her head away and stared out the small side window. "When I realized what was happening, I took some personal time. I had a lot of vacation time coming and I requested that first." Without looking in his direction, she stood to leave the cockpit and glanced down at her tattered Christmas sweater and dirty jeans. "I think I will take that shower."

Ned grabbed her arm as she swept past him and forced her to look him in the eye. "Two things. One, don't ever lie to me, and two, there's different sizes of women's clothes stashed in one of the bedroom closets if you need anything."

She tried to jerk her arm away, but he held fast.

"I haven't lied to you about anything."

"Good. Let's keep it that way. What do you do for a living, Mary Grace?"

A muscle in her jaw ticked and her eyes shifted away. He waited, wondering if she would tell the truth. Deep down, in a place he had protected for a long time, he really wanted her to be who and what she appeared to be. A sister afraid for her brother's life. Finally, she looked him straight in the eye again, this time of her own accord, and his gut told him she was being honest.

"I work for FBC, Future Broadcasting Company, as a White House press correspondent."

A big invisible fist punched Ned in the gut. A good chunk of his adult life consisted of secrets and clandestine operations. Secrets that could get people killed if they were ever exposed. He hid his unsettling reaction behind a carefully constructed mask.

Mary Grace leaned one shoulder against the doorjamb and crossed her arms over her chest. "Yeah, I didn't think you'd appreciate that little piece of information. You're a man with a belly full of secrets." She pulled away from the door frame and smiled.

Ned held his breath while he waited for the ax to fall. That smirk of hers always meant trouble.

"Do you believe in God, Ned?"

The question threw him completely off guard. He hadn't seen that one coming, but he was quick on the uptake. "Why do you ask?"

The smirk changed into a full-blown grin. "You asked me not to lie, and you better take your own advice when we get to Georgia."

He found himself intrigued, and that hadn't happened in longer than he could remember. "And why is that?"

"Because we're stopping at Gram Ramsey's house before we go to the swamp shack and my grandmother has a way of getting people to spill their guts." Her smile slid away and her eyes softened. "She's the best Christian woman I know, but—" she smiled again "—she's also one tough lady. She'll have you confessing your sins and sitting in a church pew before you can blink."

Ned scanned the cloudless day outside the front window as Mary Grace left the cockpit. The conversation left him…unsettled. He grew up in a Christian home, but he no longer believed in a God who could allow his best friend to have to live in a wheelchair for the rest of his life.

Relaxing into his chair, his lips curled into a grin as he thought about the woman he was traveling with. Maybe one day he'd tell her he owned the plane. His "hobby" as a landscape painter paid a thousand times better than the money he made working for the CIA. He put the plane on autopilot, laid his head back and allowed himself a few moments to wonder what if. What if he'd never taken that first phone call from the CIA after he left the army? What if he'd retired from the

CIA and he and Finn hadn't gone on that last mission? Everything would have been different now. He might have even been interested in asking Miss Ramsey on a date if he were a normal man, but he wasn't normal, so it was a moot point.

Opening his eyes, he switched back to manual and focused on the task at hand. It was wasted time wondering what if. A person could never go back and that was life.

Pulling out the plane's secure satellite phone, he made a call.

"'Bout time you checked in. I was starting to get worried."

Ned experienced a host of mixed emotions every time he heard Finn's voice. They had grown up together, and Ned loved him like a brother, but guilt always accompanied the affection. Ned had trusted the wrong people and Finn would pay the price for the rest of his life.

"Everything's fine. How's the new wheelchair? It's state of the art, not even on the open market yet."

A pause. "The chair's great. I appreciate it." Another longer pause. "Something's happening, isn't it? Have you caught whoever set us up?" Finn's voice was tinged with anger and hurt. Ned knew why, but it wasn't going to change anything.

"Finn, we discussed this. I don't want you involved in this hunt. You've lost too much already, and I have to live with that every day of my life."

A sulky voice responded. "You could at least tell me where you've been holed up for so long. Have you been staying on that mountain of yours?"

He no longer had to keep his location a secret, now that

he was on the move. "Yes, I've been at the cabin. I recently set it up so they'd come after me, but things changed."

He could almost feel the energy crackling to life on the other end of the phone. "What things?"

"Let's just say Bobby Lancaster went on the lam and I now have a lead on him. We've both always agreed that was the best place to start if I wasn't able to root them out without alerting them by contacting Bobby."

"Where do you think he is? Ned, please don't keep me in the dark anymore. Let me help. I have just as much invested in this as you do." He let the words linger. "Maybe more."

Ned wanted to include Finn, but his best friend had already lost too much so he ignored the heavy weight of guilt that Finn so expertly threw his way.

"I'll keep you posted and I'll have my accountant send you more money. Let me know if you need anything. Anything at all," he said, and ended the call.

A shroud of guilt lingered over him for a few minutes, but he put it away. He was doing the right thing by protecting Finn. He had stashed his best friend in a place where no one would find him until Ned discovered who wanted them dead.

The only problem was his dependence on a journalist to help him do this. If she ever got wind of some of his secrets, his life could literally blow up in his face.

SIX

Mary Grace checked out a variety of women's clothing in the huge walk-in closet in the bedroom. Either the owner of the plane was a womanizer of vast proportions or it was outfitted to carry different people. Maybe some sort of rescue transportation carrier. Her reporter's intuition indicated the latter. Just another layer of mystery surrounding Mountain Man.

Thankfully, she had an extra outfit in the backpack she'd grabbed on her way to the bathroom and had no need of the clothes. She smirked when she unzipped the pack and pulled out another Christmas sweater. She hadn't missed Ned's wary expression whenever he stared at her sweater. It only made her more curious about the man. Didn't he like Christmas?

She grinned when she passed by the king-size bed on her way to the shower. Krieger and Tink were curled up together sleeping, as if they didn't have a care in the world.

She took a quick shower, dressed and left the bathroom, dropping a kiss on her sleeping dog's snout before heading back into the main cabin. She wasn't quite ready to face Ned yet, so she started snooping around the living area. On a luxury craft like this one, there had to be hidden technology somewhere. Her heart accelerated when she plopped onto one of the buttery soft leather chairs, stared at the oblong table and noticed a thin pullout drawer beneath.

Leaning forward, she slid out what could probably also serve as an eating tray, and there sat her heart's desire. A silver gleaming laptop. Glancing toward the closed cockpit door, she opened the lid and prayed a password wasn't needed. It was already booted up, so that wasn't a problem.

She quickly typed in the home address of Ned's sister that she'd gotten off her GPS and searched the county public records for the owner's name. When the name popped up, she sat back in disgust. What in the world was RBTL Corporation? She'd never heard of them. She searched for the name on the internet but failed to get any hits. Legitimate companies usually had websites.

Pushing the laptop back underneath the table, she decided it was time to beard the lion in his lair. She snickered. Speaking of ugly beards. Her humor evaporated when she opened the door and slipped into the cockpit. A sleek little laptop, similar to the one she had just been working on, sat on the console between the pilot and copilot's seat. The screen was turned toward the door revealing the address she had just visited on the other computer. Avoiding eye contact, she slipped into the copilot's seat.

"Snooping again, Miss Ramsey?" he asked after eyeing her sweater with something akin to horror.

A streak of anger shot through her system, along with a bit of embarrassment at getting caught red-handed, but then she shrugged. She was a reporter, after all. It was her job to snoop.

"You only call me Miss Ramsey when you're aggravated. The name's Mary Grace."

She slipped him a glance. He had a smile on his face and it disarmed her. No! No way was she allowing herself to be attracted to no-last-name Ned—a man with the word *secret* emblazoned on his chest.

Back to business. "I assume there's a sat phone on-board?"

He reached down, opened a hidden compartment and handed her the plane's phone. She gave him a sharp look, but grabbed it out of his hand. "I thought I'd try my brother again. I doubt I'll get an answer, but it's worth a try."

He gave a slight nod. "Just don't reveal our destination."

She nodded and punched in the number from memory, counting four rings before the voice mail recording came on. "Bobby, please, if you get this message, call me. I located Mountain Man." She wanted to say more, tell Bobby that even though she wanted to kill him, she loved him more than anything, but since Ned was listening to every word, she ended the call.

Lost in thought and worried sick about her brother, Mary Grace stared out the front window of the plane. She prayed Bobby was holed up at the swamp shack. When they were kids, they'd trekked through the woods to the abandoned cabin hidden a little ways into the Okefenokee Swamp. As far as she knew, no one was aware of the place. In all the years they went there, nothing indicated anyone else hanging around. Anyone visiting the swamp tended to take the offered tours and stay within the strict, designated pedestrian areas. In the past, people had disappeared in the 438,000 acres of wetland.

Lost in her thoughts, it took a moment for Ned's question to penetrate her brain.

"What?"

"If he's on the run, do you really expect Bobby to answer his phone? If we're right, I'm sure there are people trying to track him."

A picture of her blue-eyed, fair-haired brother formed in her mind and she shuddered at the thought of him on his own, trying to outrun a bunch of killers. "He is in cyber intelligence. I was hoping he could figure out a way for me to get in touch with him."

"I know a thing or two about technology and I don't think your brother would take a chance by using his phone. That's the first thing he would have ditched."

Mary Grace slumped in her seat. If Bobby wasn't at the old cabin, she didn't know where else to look. They would have to wait for him to contact her. That didn't sit well because she was used to plowing forward and making things happen.

"You know I'm a reporter." It wasn't a question.

"An unfortunate circumstance, but yes, you shared that nice little tidbit of information with me earlier."

She cut him a sharp look. "My job is not a crime and there's no need to be sarcastic."

"I apologize. Now, why did you bring up that disturbing information again?"

A small twinkle in his eye revealed that he was baiting her. She refused to give him the satisfaction.

"My point is that I'm very good at what I do, and I have quite a few contacts in Washington. If you'd tell me what you think Bobby has done to you and your friend, Finn, maybe I can help. You know, dig up some information."

The twinkle disappeared and his green eyes took on the unyielding substance of emeralds. "If the situation turns out to be explosive, will you write a story and tell the world what is happening, even if it disrupts and maybe even places people's lives in danger?"

"You go too far, Mountain Man. I would never knowingly place someone in danger."

From one second to the next, Ned's body relaxed and he nodded at the sat phone in her lap. "I suggest you call your grandmother. Let her know we're coming and make sure she's okay."

Mary Grace's heart almost exploded inside her chest when the meaning of his words sank in. "What do you mean, *make sure she's okay*?" But deep down she knew what he meant and reprimanded herself for not thinking of it earlier. If the people after her and Bobby went to Georgia looking for them, they'd find Gram Ramsey.

Fumbling, she almost dropped the phone before she got the number dialed. Her grandmother answered on the third ring and Mary Grace's heart settled back into a regular rhythm. Gram was safe. For the moment.

Ned hardened his heart against Mary Grace's apparent love for her grandmother. Just because she adored her gram didn't mean she wouldn't use him and his circumstances to further her career. He'd never been exposed to many reporters because he'd always stayed as far away from them as possible. He had a cache of hidden secrets, in both his personal and professional life, and he never ever wanted them exposed to the world.

He only halfway listened to Mary Grace's conversation with her grandmother and waited until she disconnected the call. "Everything okay?"

Her tortured gaze met his. "For now. I tried to talk her into staying with one of her bridge partners until we arrive, but she wouldn't hear of it. Said she'd spent every night in that house since Grampy died and no ill-mannered thugs were going to force her to leave."

"Sounds like your grandparents loved each other."

Her lips curled into a half smile and Ned wasn't happy that his heart pinged in gladness when the worry lines on her forehead disappeared. Not a good sign.

"They did. In their own way. Gram is the epitome of Georgian hospitality and tradition. I think my grandfather somewhat resented Gram's family. She inherited her family home—the Hubert House—and they lived there after they got married."

"The Hubert House?" Mary Grace was turning out to be a fount of information. He grinned and it felt good. Too good.

"Only the historic houses have names, and Hubert is Gram's maiden name—the house has been in her family for generations, but back to Grampy. He wasn't as high on the social ladder as Gram, and all those years ago, that was a big deal. It didn't help that he couldn't handle money well. Gram still lives in the house, but she really doesn't have enough cash to keep it up as it should be."

Mary Grace went quiet for a moment and Ned caught a look of nostalgia on her face.

"You still worried about your gram?"

She shrugged, but Ned could tell something was bothering her. She peered out the side window of the plane and continued talking. "Gram was an only child. My mother was her only child and I'm Gram's only blood-related grandchild."

"And?"

When she turned around, the sadness in her gaze caught him off guard. He wanted to slay dragons if that's what it took to remove that emotion.

"Gram is leaving Hubert House to me. She doesn't trust Mom not to sell it. She hopes I'll get married one day and fill it with children and happiness."

His gut clenched at the thought of Mary Grace married with children, but he gritted his teeth and spoke as if no emotion had touched him. Something he was good at.

"Maybe that'll happen."

She turned away again. "Let's just say I come from the epitome of a dysfunctional family and it hasn't helped in the relationship department. But you don't want to hear about my sordid childhood. All you're interested in is locating Bobby and attaining whatever information he has." She turned and gave him a hard look. "Right?"

His heart wanted to protest her statement, but his brain conquered the momentary glitch.

"Right."

"Well, hopefully we'll find Bobby, you'll see that he is completely innocent and I'll be out of your hair for good."

Silence filled the cockpit and Ned's curiosity got the

best of him. He tried to convince himself that the more he knew about Mary Grace and Bobby, the better his interrogation of her brother would go, but he also had a burning desire to gather every tidbit of information he could muster from the woman sitting next to him.

"You want to know more about me? How about we trade information?"

Her golden eyes reflected the intensity of a tiger on the hunt and he almost regretted the offer. Almost. But he was a master at revealing vague information that could never be researched and analyzed.

She fired a shot at him immediately and the question surprised him.

"Which side of the family did you get your height from? You're what, six and a half feet tall?"

He held back a grin. At least she wasn't worried about her grandmother for the moment.

"Got my height from Dad's side of the family, and yes, I'm six feet six inches. My turn."

She leaned back in her seat and grinned, anticipation of the verbal battle lighting her eyes. It was the first time he'd seen a genuine smile and he took a hard punch to the gut, but quickly tamped down the emotion.

"Go for it. Unlike you, I have nothing to hide."

He fired a volley. "Exactly how many relationships have you tried that went bad?" He wanted to sew his mouth shut after the question passed his lips, but he really wanted to know why her relationships never worked out.

"Three."

Ned didn't miss the dispassionate way she answered. He detected a world of hurt hidden behind her short, clipped response.

It was her turn to ask, "You don't wear a ring. Are you, or have you ever been, married?"

"That's two questions, but the answer is no, and no. What made you want to become a journalist?"

She paused and a thoughtful expression blanketed her face. He liked that she didn't give a status quo answer.

"I found my niche in high school when I joined the school newspaper. We published it once a month and I quickly became hooked. I discovered that the pen actually is mightier than the sword. I exposed bullies and all sorts of injustices that teenagers have to live with. I also got to report on the happier achievements of students. I loved it and still do."

Ned heard and greedily absorbed every detail of what she said, but he caught movement in the sky out of the corner of his eye.

"We have company. Go to the back and buckle yourself into one of the seats."

"No can do, Mountain Man," she said as she tightened the buckle on the copilot's seat. "You might need me."

It didn't surprise him that the spirited woman sitting next to him refused to take orders, but he didn't have time to worry about it.

"In that case, brace yourself. There's a drone closing in on us and it's locked and loaded."

Instead of doing what any normal person would have done to protect themselves, she chose to argue. "That's impossible. I recently did a story on the rights of private citizens to shoot down drones that hover over their house, which, by the way, several states have now allowed, but there aren't any drones on the market, even military ones, that can keep up with a jet."

Ned banked the jet hard to the right and gritted his teeth. He had no doubt the thing was going to shoot at them. "That's because they've kept it a well-guarded secret. The Pentagon is close to releasing what they call the UTAP-22. The thing can fly seven hundred miles an hour and is loaded with a lethal mix of weapons. Looks like someone either stole the specs and built their own, or this thing we're involved in goes all the way to the top of the food chain."

The drone caught up with them and was keeping pace with his side window. "Hold tight!" he yelled.

SEVEN

Mary Grace's hands clenched the arms of her seat when the drone came alongside their jet. The thing was large but had a toylike appearance, at least until the bottom doors opened and a small bomb fell into the air.

"Ned?" she choked out.

He didn't answer, but kept one hand on the yoke while typing furiously on the still-open laptop on the console with the other.

"Ned!" she shrieked. "What are you doing? You're typing and we're about to be blown to smithereens."

"I have this," he said calmly.

She stared, mesmerized, as the small bomb chased them through the air and Ned banked the jet sharply to the right. The missile came within inches of hitting the plane before suddenly making a sharp turn back toward the drone. She held tight as Ned shifted their plane once again, and then understood why when the drone exploded into tiny little pieces.

Everything happened so fast it took Mary Grace several seconds to come out of her frozen state. "Wh-what just happened?" She gazed into his electric green eyes, alive with the excitement of battle, and shivered again.

"Who are you?" she whispered.

He sighed and gripped the yoke of the plane harder. "I'm just a man trying to survive and see that justice is done. Listen, I own this plane. I hacked into the drone and turned the missile back on itself."

Mary Grace closed her eyes, said a prayer of thanks for the good Lord sparing their lives, then turned and looked at Ned. It was time to play hardball. "Here's the deal. We're going to part ways when this airplane lands if you don't tell me what's going on, and I mean everything." She held her breath and allowed her words to linger in the air.

He stared at the clear blue sky in front of them before shifting his gaze to hers. His hands finally relaxed, as if he had come to a decision.

"I'll tell you everything on two conditions."

She took a hard swallow. This was going to be a tough one, she knew it in her gut. "I'm listening."

"First, anything you find out about my personal life and identity is to be kept private, and if your brother is culpable, in any way, you won't interfere while I make sure he's prosecuted to the fullest extent of the law."

This was the warrior she'd caught glimpses of while at the cabin. His voice had hardened to a degree she hadn't heard before and she knew he meant serious business. Well, so did she.

"I have two conditions of my own," she snapped back. "Before any authorities are called in, I insist you have rock-solid evidence that Bobby did something wrong. Also, if, and this is a big if, Bobby was somehow involved in what happened, someone could have set him up. I want you to listen to what he has to say, if we find him, and follow up on all the information he gives us before you make that final decision. And I also want your identity verified by someone official. Someone I can trust."

His lips curved upward at the sides and it threw her off guard.

"I like your style, Mary Grace, and I admire your loyalty to your brother. I'll give him every opportunity to prove his innocence." He took the satellite phone from her hands and grinned before pressing a button. "This is Ned. I need to speak with her."

Curiosity was eating Mary Grace alive, but she stayed quiet and waited, a professional journalist at her best.

Someone on the other end of the line must have picked up. "It's Ned. I'll fill you in later. I need you to verify to someone that I'm one of the good guys. You know her. Mary Grace Ramsey. She's a White House press correspondent for FBC."

Mary Grace heard the person on the other end of the phone line raise their voice and she leaned close, straining to hear.

Ned grinned at her and she snapped back in her seat.

"She won't be a problem. I'll make sure of it."

He handed the phone to her and she grabbed it out of his hand before placing it close to her ear.

"This is Mary Grace Ramsey," she said in a crisp, professional voice.

A woman chuckled on the other end of the line and it stunned Mary Grace for a moment. "I can tell from your tone you've been around Ned for too long. The boy has the social skills of a bull in a china shop."

A herd of wild horses kicked up a storm in her gut and Mary Grace swallowed the lump in her throat when she recognized the voice on the other end of the line. She had thrown more than her share of questions at CIA Director Madeline Cooper in her role as a journalist.

"Ma'am I apologize for interrupting your day, but I'm in a situation here and I need to know I can trust the man sitting next to me."

A weary sigh reached her ears. "I have no idea what's going on, but yes, you can trust Ned with your life." Madeline Cooper cleared her throat and transformed into the powerful, no-nonsense leader she was widely known to be. "But I want to make one thing clear. There will be no cooperation from this department on a story unless it's approved by me first due to potentially classified information. Do we have an understanding?"

Mary Grace backed down, but she had one more question. "Yes, ma'am. Understood. One more thing. What's Ned's full name?"

The CIA director laughed out loud. "You're a journalist. I'll leave that for you to discover," she said, and the line went dead.

Mary Grace mimicked Tinker Bell when she was in a bad mood, giving Ned the whale eye. "You could have warned me it was Madeline Cooper."

He laughed, and for some reason, Mary Grace got a toasty warm feeling because she had been the one to make him smile.

"And spoil all the fun?" He glanced at her. "You satisfied?"

She grinned back at him. "For the moment. And now

that negotiations are complete, it's time for you to fess up and tell me everything that's going on."

That wiped the smile off his face. She mourned the loss for a moment, but reminded herself that Bobby's freedom, and both their lives, were at stake.

"Aye, it's time." He hesitated, then gave her a rueful grin. "I'm not used to sharing information, so bear with me."

Mary Grace snorted. "You're a regular vault, all locked up tight as a drum. Just tell me already. It's not going to kill you." Her curiosity was on overload.

"You already know about my time in the army. After two years, I ended up in Special Forces and four years later, I'd had enough of the seedier side of human nature, so Krieger and I mustered out."

A thousand questions were already racing through her mind. "Did you have any trouble getting the dog out? I know a trained military dog is expensive."

The ferocious expression on his face had her leaning back in her seat.

"I had to jump through a dozen hoops to get the dog released into my custody, but Krieger was coming home with me, regardless. He saved my life multiple times."

Ned's love, passion and respect for Krieger shone in his eyes. Mary Grace didn't doubt for a second that he would have done just about anything to keep his dog with him.

"Let's just say, I agreed to make a hefty donation to the dog training program and let it go at that."

She nodded and he went on. "My best friend, Finn Lachlan, joined the army when I did, and we worked well together. We were assigned to the same unit. My team made a name for ourselves within the military and political community. We handled a lot of dicey international situations the government wanted kept quiet. About six months after we both got out of the army, I received a call from the CIA director asking if Finn and I would come to work for her. We agreed as long as we could work together. Over a period of several years, we slipped in and out of places and gathered information. Nothing really dangerous."

"Why did she want you and your friend, Finn, so badly?" She was almost sure she heard his teeth grind.

"I have dual citizenship. My mom is American and my dad is from Scotland. Due to my family's vocation, we traveled all over the world and I learned to speak many languages. I can move in and out of a lot of countries with ease."

That could mean anything from his being a military brat to the son of the rich and famous, which, by looking at him, she highly doubted, but the luxurious plane confused things. His appearance and presentation didn't mesh with the jet.

"And your family's vocation is?"

He raised a bushy brow, ignored her question and kept talking. "The last job Finn and I handled went bad. It took me a while to piece together what happened, but I finally realized we were set up. I have absolute trust in Madeline Cooper, who has nothing to gain by setting us up. We were given bad intel and were ambushed." He gave her a dark look. "Intel, in part, given to us by your brother."

Shock reverberated through her. "Bobby doesn't

work with field agents. He's a computer analyst. He gathers information and passes it on to his superiors."

He would wear his molars out at the rate he was grinding his teeth, but then he shot her a look of pity. Mary Grace seethed. She had gotten enough of those glances growing up when all the other kids in school teased her about her mother and stepfather.

"Sounds to me like your sweet, innocent brother hasn't shared everything with you."

Fury tore through her and her professionalism plummeted. Now *she* was gritting her teeth. "Maybe, just maybe, the CIA didn't allow him to tell me what he was doing. You ever think of that? Bobby is innocent and I'll prove it. Now tell me why Finn joined you at the CIA. Seems to me after years in the army, you both would have had enough of warfare."

He cast her a wary glance, then shrugged nonchalantly. Maybe a little too casually? Her gut told her he was only planning to reveal parts of the story, but she waited for his answer. She had learned a long time ago to give the interviewee time to trip themselves up, but it was obvious that Ned measured and weighed every tiny morsel of information he begrudgingly parted with.

"Finn and I were a team. If she wanted my services, they included Finn, and Finn needed the money."

So now she knew Finn was financially insecure. She briefly wondered if Ned needed the income, too, but quickly discarded the idea based on what she knew of him.

"It was supposed to be an easy in and out. Our job was to attend an art show at a famous gallery, pose as art dealers, get into the owner's office and download everything on his computer. The owner of the gallery had political ties and shipped art worldwide. He was suspected of hiding state secrets and information in the shipments. Our government wanted a list of his shipments."

"Why not just hack into his computer and get what they wanted?"

"In today's environment, people with something to hide usually have two systems. One for their normal work, and the other they never connect online. It's for their eyes only."

Mary Grace had to admit she'd never thought of that. "So you and Finn went in to download whatever was on the second computer. What happened, then?"

His hands tightened on the yoke again and Mary Grace rubbed her throat. She could easily visualize those large strong hands wrapping around someone's throat and squeezing the life out of them, but then she remembered how gentle and kind Ned had been with his niece and she dropped her hand and relaxed.

"It was an ambush. Finn went in to do the download and I waited just outside the door to make sure no one came down the hall. I heard a scuffle and entered the room, but it was too late. There was an open window in the office and a man dressed head-to-toe in black disappeared through the opening. I barely got a glimpse of him. I couldn't pursue because Finn was down."

He stopped for a moment, but Mary Grace knew better than to offer the comfort she so desperately wanted to. He thought her brother was somehow responsible for this horrific event. But that was impossible. Wasn't it? No, Bobby would never do anything like that.

"The guy used a silencer and the bullet hit Finn in the spine, disabling him for life." Her heart went out to him. She didn't want to ask the question burning a hole in her gut, but she forced her lips to move. "And what makes you think Bobby had something to do with the ambush?"

He looked at her and his emerald eyes turned molten. "Because Bobby was responsible for monitoring all movement and information of the enemy. He gave me the all-clear signal. There were cameras inside the office and he had hacked into them. He had to know those two men were lying in wait. I couldn't do two things at once and had to rely on the CIA team members to do the hacking and monitoring."

Ned's explanation shook Mary Grace to the core. She kept her expression even, but her heart was about to pound out of her chest. She breathed slowly through her nose until she calmed down enough to think. Pushing aside the churning, turbulent emotions connected to her brother, she forced herself to think like the reporter she was.

Mary Grace knew Bobby inside and out, but since working at the CIA, she noticed he'd become quieter, which she'd chalked up to maturity. She closed her eyes and let her mind rest for a second, clearing her thoughts. She popped upright when possible explanations presented themselves.

"You said yourself that Bobby hacked into the cameras in that man's office. What if someone else overrode Bobby's computer and the picture showed the room clear?" She gave a thoughtful pause. "Sounds to me like there might be some corruption going on."

He cut her a sharp look. "Aye, the corruption might begin with your brother, but there's someone more powerful behind him, pulling the strings. He should be able to lead me to them."

EIGHT

Ned only had a moment's respite before Mary Grace surprised him with her next question.

"Tell me about your friend, Finn."

"His name is Finn Lachlan. He's a natural born American citizen with a Scottish heritage. My family traveled a lot, but our home base is in the States. Finn and I were best friends growing up. He followed me into the army, and after that, as I told you, we joined the CIA."

"You feel responsible for his injury."

He took a deep breath and calmed the emotions churning in his gut.

"I don't see how that's pertinent to our current situation." His words sounded gruff and irritable, but he didn't really care.

She wouldn't find much information on his old friend because he'd made sure both his and Finn's operational backgrounds were buried deep. She might be a good, even great, reporter, but with his experience he had no doubt he could run information rings around her.

But he was curious. "Why ask me about Finn?"

She casually peered out the side window, but the tension in her body told a different story.

"Curiosity. That's all." The tone of her voice said differently.

"Tell me." It came out as a command, but at this point he really didn't care. He wanted to know what was going on in that active, inquisitive mind of hers.

She turned toward him and looked him in the eye. "Do you trust Finn?"

His gut rolled over once before the anger hit him. "What are you implying? Finn was the one left disabled for life. I grew up with him. Of course I trust him."

"Sorry to hit a nerve." She shrugged. "I'm a reporter. My job is to ask questions. If you say you trust Finn, fine, I believe you. Just covering all the bases."

He forced himself to calm down. She was right. It was her job to ask questions and probe for information and he'd do well to remember that. He needed a break from her inquisition and realized he could smell himself. He stunk.

"Listen, I'm going to take a quick shower and change clothes. I'll put the plane on autopilot. Call me if anything buzzes or sounds wrong." He grinned to himself as he pushed out of the pilot's chair and headed toward the door. Mary Grace didn't know he had a plane-wide computer system that would alert him if there were any problems. That included notifications of any unwanted visitors like the drone that had visited them earlier.

A big grin split his face and he kept walking when she screeched at his back.

"What? You can't just leave me here. What if someone tries to attack us again? What am I supposed to do? What if we have engine trouble?"

It got even worse when she realized he wasn't coming back. "I'm never flying with you again, you hear me? You're a crazy mountain man."

He scratched the scraggly beard covering his face and decided it was time to get rid of it. It had been functional on the cold mountain, but they were headed to Georgia. As he passed the plush seats in the middle of the plane, he wondered what Mary Grace would think of his clean-shaven face. Not that it mattered. As soon as he ran Bobby to ground and squeezed every morsel of information out of him, Ned would disappear. He wouldn't be seeing Mary Grace again.

His heart missed a beat at the thought of never peering into those intelligent golden eyes again, but he had a personal mission. Ned wanted to find the person responsible for putting Finn in a wheelchair and destroying his friend's life.

He shook his head when he entered the bedroom and spotted Krieger protectively curled around TB. The unlikely friendship between two such different dogs reminded him just how different he and Mary Grace were. He had tons of secrets and she was in the business of revealing them.

He grabbed a pair of worn comfy jeans and a soft blue jean shirt, but paused with the clothes in his hands and stared at the neatly laundered khakis and starched shirts. He threw the clothes back into the closet and removed a pair of pants and a shirt from their hangers. Mary Grace's grandmother sounded old school and he wanted to make a good impression. He had a gift for being able to fit into any environment and social situation.

He headed toward the shower and worked hard to convince himself that shaving his beard and dressing nicely had nothing to do with Mary Grace. Nope, this was all about information gathering. It didn't have a thing to do with the gorgeous, terrified, sassy woman currently sitting in the copilot's seat of his plane.

Fuming, and somewhat terrified to be the only person in the cockpit of a large airplane—although she'd never admit that to Ned—Mary Grace sat there and stared at the panel full of instruments, her fingers gripping the armrests. Every one of them was completely foreign to her. If something happened, they'd just have to crash while Mr. Mountain-Man-No-Last-Name-Ned took his leisurely shower.

Loosening her grip on the armrest, she started tapping her fingers against the leather while her brain began functioning again. She relaxed when she realized that a plane this equipped most likely had a computer system that would alert Ned if any problems presented themselves. No pilot on a commercial plane would ever leave the cockpit, except to use the bathroom, and they had copilots.

She grinned. Ned had a warped sense of humor and she liked it, maybe a little too much. He cared about and helped his friend, Finn, and had a burning desire to root out the bad guys. The only problem was that it might be at her brother's expense. Her momentary fuzzy feelings took a sharp nosedive at that thought.

Mary Grace would protect her brother with her last

breath and Ned was convinced Bobby had something to do with the ambush the two men experienced.

Her nails tapped harder against the arm of her seat as she thought through everything Ned had shared. He'd been very careful to keep his personal life concealed. He'd told her about the ambush, who he and Finn had worked for and that was it. What interested her the most outside of Ned's unknown personal history was the fact that Ned and Finn worked for the CIA.

That type of story was right down her alley, but her first priority was to find and protect her brother. Lost in her own thoughts, she jumped when Ned spoke from the entrance of the cockpit.

"Man, that shower felt great. I didn't realize how filthy I was."

"Yeah, well, I wasn't going to say anything, but…"

Her words fell away and her chin dropped when she swiveled around in her seat and got her first real look at Ned. The nasty beard had disappeared, only to reveal a granite-sharp jawline. The skin on the lower portion of his face was lighter than the upper portion due to the beard, but the man could easily be on the cover of a sports magazine, any sports magazine. He had on khakis and a starched button-down shirt with the sleeves rolled up, revealing muscled forearms.

The man was drop-dead gorgeous, and before she could clamp her lips shut, the words popped out of her mouth. "Are you sure you're not married?"

Those intelligent emerald eyes sparked with humor and Mary Grace wanted to crawl under the seat.

"That's not what I meant to say," she blurted out

again. This was going from bad to worse. She took a deep breath and pasted on a false smile.

"I meant to say you clean up pretty good."

Grinning, he slid into the pilot's chair and checked all the controls. She wanted to smack the smile off his face because it was at her expense. She looked away, but couldn't stop from sneaking another peek. Mountain Man really was too good-looking for his own good. The guy probably had a woman stashed in every country. He certainly had the means to travel extensively with his expensive plane.

"I'm really glad you didn't touch anything while I was gone."

An explosion welled up inside her, but he grinned at her again before she had a chance to erupt.

"And once again, no, I promise I've never been married."

With stiff shoulders, she shrugged in embarrassment. Immense relief hit her in waves when he changed the subject.

"We'll be landing within twenty minutes. Buckle yourself in."

Mary Grace pulled the seat belt across her chest, her mind shifting to her grandmother. She prayed that the older lady was safe and the killer hadn't decided to pay her a visit, trying to find Bobby. Gram Ramsey might be tough, but she wouldn't stand a chance against the people after them.

NINE

After a perfect landing, Ned guided the plane behind a large building, which effectively shielded the aircraft from unwanted eyes. He flipped a bunch of switches and the engine rumbled off. He bit back a grin when Mary Grace slowly relaxed the death grip she had on the armrests.

"I didn't know this airstrip was here and I've lived in this area all my life." Those golden eyes of hers gazed at him, full of curiosity and suspicion.

He shrugged. "It's a privately owned airstrip. There's hundreds of them across the United States. Most owners will allow usage for the right price."

The gold band around the brown in her eyes burned bright with righteousness. "Does that mean bad, as well as good, people can pay for usage?"

He shrugged again. "If you don't like it, do a story on it."

Standing, she straightened her sweater and Ned winced. Most Christmas sweaters weren't very pretty, but this new one was much worse than the previous one she'd been wearing. It was green with a triangular

Christmas tree on the front. Sewn in ornaments were placed all over it and yarn tassels flowed free from the top of several of them.

"I'll do that. We should get going. I'm worried about Gram Ramsey."

He understood her concern. He had a crotchety old grandfather he worried about all the time. Angus Duncan, laird of their family clan in Scotland, did his best to interfere in Ned's life, but he loved the old man dearly.

By the time he left the cockpit, Mary Grace and the two dogs were impatiently waiting on him by the exit door. She had her backpack slung over one shoulder and TB was safely ensconced in the dog carrier strapped to her chest.

She caught his scowl as she looked up from fiddling with the straps of the dog carrier. "What?"

"You shouldn't be carrying all that gear with the wound in your side."

She shot him a feral grin and the backpack slid from her shoulder and plunked onto the carpeted floor. "I'll be happy for you to carry my stuff."

He scowled again for good measure. Aye, the woman was as surly and stubborn as the pony he'd had as a kid. "Let me grab my gear and we'll be on our way."

He strode to the back of the plane to the bedroom, opened a hidden closet panel and grabbed the duffel bag that was always packed and ready to go at a moment's notice. He was back at her side in moments. He pressed the release hatch button and the stairs lowered to the ground.

He grinned at Mary Grace's back as she quickly scaled the steps and took a relieved breath when her feet hit the ground. His scowl returned when Krieger followed along behind, instead of in front of, the woman and her rat dog like a mutt in love. He was trained to leave the plane first and check the perimeter.

"Krieger, perimeter." He snapped out the order and Mary Grace frowned over her shoulder, her gaze following Krieger as the dog disappeared around the corner of the building.

Carrying his duffel and her backpack, he took the steps two at a time and stopped at her side, waiting for his dog to give the all-clear.

TB stuck her head out of the pouch and Mary Grace soothed the rat dog by stroking her gently on the head and making nonsensical noises when the dog started whining. She looked up at Ned with amusement lighting her eyes and his heart expanded in his chest. It disgruntled him that a mere look from this woman— a journalist at that—could make him react in such an unsettling fashion.

"What?" he snapped, then felt like a fool for allowing emotions to get in the way of the important task at hand.

She grinned wider and he felt as if she could somehow see inside him, past the gruff exterior and hard shell he'd grown.

"I think Krieger's in love with Tinker Bell."

"What? That's preposterous."

Mary Grace tilted her head and her eyes became mere slits. "You think just because Krieger is a fully trained dog that he's too good for my Tinker Bell?"

Ned became very wary. His grandfather always said that women would say one thing and mean something else entirely. That a man had to pay close attention to figure out what was really going on. He was terrified that she wasn't talking about dogs, but alluding to something much more personal, so he took a relieved breath when Krieger came loping around the corner of the building and sat in front of him, giving the all-clear signal. He ignored her question and moved forward. "Let's go."

Handled by his contact, an empty car sat in front of the small building that manned the airport, waiting on them. A man inside the building threw his hand up but turned away when they approached the car. Mary Grace pinned him with a look brimming with questions, but opened the back door for Krieger, closed it and loaded herself and TB into the passenger seat.

He held her backpack out to her, which she took and placed on the floorboard, then tossed his duffel into the back seat. She didn't say a word until he pulled out his phone and asked for the address of her grandmother's house. He input the information she relayed, backed the car out of the parking space and they were on their way. He didn't have to wait long for the explosion of questions.

"I don't see how we were able to land at that airstrip without filing a proper flight plan. And how we were able to bypass security at the airport. We've probably broken a ton of laws, and if I get into trouble, it's going to be your fault. And why didn't you use the GPS in the car?"

His head pounded as her questions peppered him like a round of gunfire. "Everything we've done has been legally authorized. You won't get in trouble." Then understanding dawned. "You're a stickler for the rules, aren't you?"

She sniffed in disdain. "Rules are there for a reason. What would society look like if we didn't have rules?"

He snorted in disbelief. Mary Grace was a White House press correspondent. She was exposed to the underbelly of Washington politics on a daily basis. She should have known better.

"In a perfect world, if everyone played by the rules, then the government wouldn't need people like me. Someone has to be there to clean up the mess everyone else makes of their lives and their countries."

"You're very cynical, you know that?"

His lips twisted in the parody of a smile. "Yes, I'm cynical to the core, and with good reason. Someone, likely from my own country, betrayed me and Finn and I'll not rest until I track them down and they're rotting behind bars."

Ned ignored the fact that Mary Grace had reiterated what his own family had been telling him. He refused to let anything get in the way of justice, and that included the woman sitting closed-mouth—for the first time since he'd met her—in the seat beside him. Nothing more was said until they pulled into the driveway of her grandmother's house.

With the car still idling, Mary Grace instructed Ned to crack the windows for the dogs and then sat staring at the house that became a refuge during her turbulent teenage years. Not only for her, but for Bobby, too. Just like the old house, now decked out in Christmas finery, Gram Ramsey had wrapped both of the lonely, bewildered kids in her loving arms and practically raised them herself while her mother and stepfather were gambling their way to destitution. And now she and Bobby had possibly placed her in danger.

After removing Tinker Bell from her pouch and placing her in the back seat with Krieger, she reached for the door handle.

"Impressive place."

Trying to see it fresh, through Ned's eyes, Mary Grace stared at the historical Greek Revival–style home, supported by four large round columns holding up the front porch ceiling. Two expanded windows were placed on either side of the half-glassed front door, and six regular-sized windows marched across the top. A set of six steps, sided with brick and flared out on each side, led to the porch.

The swing she had sat in as a teenager, dreaming about her future, still hung by two chains attached to the two-story porch ceiling. Gram Ramsey had shared many pearls of wisdom with Mary Grace in that swing. Two huge Christmas wreaths adorned each side of the tall historical two-door entrance. Greenery lovingly wrapped itself around the columns, each one with a big red bow at the top. Mary Grace had inherited her grandmother's love of Christmas adornment, but Gram made sure she and Bobby understood the true meaning of Christmas and everything it represented. Mary Grace had decorated her town house, but it never felt the same as Hubert House, the only place that was truly home.

But if a person bothered to look closer, and she had no doubt that eagle-eyed Ned would, there were small signs of neglect. A little paint peeling here and there, shrubs that needed trimming. Her heart clinched at the thought of the grand old place going downhill due to lack of funds, but her grandmother was a proud woman. Mary Grace had offered to help as much as she was able with the upkeep, but Gram Ramsey wouldn't hear of it.

Mary Grace turned the car door handle and pushed open the door. "Yeah, well, if I have anything to do with it, it'll stay that way, at least until Gram Ramsey goes to meet her Maker."

She heard the smile in his words when he asked, "Goes to meet her Maker?"

She twisted around, filled with comical anticipation. "Oh, I'm sure by the time we leave you'll understand all about meeting your Maker."

His grin slid away, replaced by a frown, but she swung her legs out of the car and landed on her feet. She wanted to see for herself that Gram was okay. She heard the driver's car door shut behind her, but she ignored Ned's order to wait on him and ran up the steps she'd run up hundreds of times. He caught up with her, grabbed the front door handle before she could reach it and shoved her behind him.

"It's safer for me to go in first."

Raising both hands in the air, she grinned. "By all means, be my guest, but I'd be careful if I were you."

He was still turned, staring at her, when the door jerked inward and out of his grasp. Mary Grace's grin widened at his expression of sheer amazement when he froze at the sound of a shotgun being cocked with the experience of a seasoned hunter. Without taking her eyes off Ned, she said, "It's okay, Gram, he's with me."

When the trigger made a sound, releasing the hammer and uncocking the gun, Ned let loose a pent-up breath and shot Mary Grace a dark look, silently promising retribution.

Mary Grace slapped a hand over her mouth to stop from laughing and sidled around him so she wouldn't miss anything as Ned slowly turned to face his adversary. He had to keep lowering his chin until he caught sight of her proud five-foot-two-inches-tall grandmother. She probably weighed in at a whopping ninety pounds, but she held the rifle with authority.

With gentility and grace, Gram Ramsey propped the rifle against the foyer wall and greeted her guest with all the aplomb of a Southern belle, as if she'd never pointed a rifle in his face.

"Mary Grace, child, you get over here right now and give your grandmother a big hug, then you can introduce me properly to your young man."

She stepped forward and hugged the small woman fiercely. A sense of peace and love enveloped her. Gram Ramsey had been the only stabilizing force in Mary Grace's life and she loved the older woman with all her heart. Pulling back, she studied Gram closely. She visited as often as she could, but it was never enough. Her grandmother looked a little older every time she came home. She'd been joking with Ned, but she couldn't stand to think of Gram *actually* meeting her Maker.

Feeling a huge relief that her grandmother was okay, Mary Grace waved a hand toward Ned. "He's not my young man. We only recently met. This is Ned. As I explained on the phone, we're looking for Bobby and some disreputable people are trailing us."

Gram gave her a sharp look. Mary Grace knew what

it meant and she shrugged her shoulders. "He won't tell me his last name, so I can't introduce him properly." Inwardly, she smiled. She doubted Ned had ever met anyone like her grandmother. With a warm Southern smile and gracious manners, Gram could perform an interrogation that would make the military sit up and take notice.

Gram stepped closer to Ned and touched his arm in a friendly fashion, but the light of battle and determination lit her eyes in a way Mary Grace hadn't seen in a long time. There was something else in her grandmother's eyes. Something Mary Grace would put a stop to as soon as she got her grandmother alone. Gram Ramsey was envied in the community for her matchmaking skills, and Mary Grace didn't want her to get anything in her head about her and Ned.

"Well, then, Ned, my name is Athena Hubert Ramsey. Athena comes from my mother's side of the family, you know. I'd like to welcome you to Hubert House and I'd dearly love to know your surname so I can address you properly."

It was almost comical watching the hulking man hover nervously over her tiny grandmother, but he finally grimaced and spouted forcefully, "Nolan Eli Duncan, ma'am, and I would appreciate it if you wouldn't spread that around." He glanced at the plethora of decorations and a small Christmas tree that Gram always placed in the foyer before his gaze landed back on Gram, and he said in a nervous rush, as if trying to make conversation, "I see where Mary Grace gets her love of Christmas."

Ned stole a small piece of Mary Grace's heart when

he nervously addressed her grandmother, and her heart warmed when her grandmother patted his large muscular arm. Then it dawned on her, Nolan Eli Duncan was long for Ned.

"Now that wasn't so hard, was it?" Gram said, then started spewing orders like a miniature drill sergeant. "Mary Grace, bring young Eli into the parlor to meet the ladies, then you can show him to his room. I'm sure you two would like to freshen up."

Mary Grace quickly moved past the fact that she now knew Ned's name—if that was his real name—and grimaced before laying a hand on her grandmother's arm. "Gram, we can't stay. I came to make sure you're okay and to ask again if you'd be willing to stay with one of your friends until we find Bobby and get this matter resolved. This is the first place the people after us will come looking for him. It's easy to find out Bobby and I pretty much grew up here."

Gram reared back and assessed Ned from head to toe. "Eli, I won't ask about the particulars of this situation, but can I trust you to keep my granddaughter safe?"

Mary Grace stifled a grin when he bobbed his head like a schoolboy being caught with his hand in the cookie jar. "I'll do my best, ma'am."

Gram nodded. "That's all I can ask." She turned toward Mary Grace and held her arms wide. "Come give an old lady another hug." Mary Grace walked into her arms. "I'll be praying for you, child," she whispered into her ear. "And I like your young man. The good Lord brought him into your life for a reason only He knows. Have patience."

Mary Grace didn't have a chance to ask what her grandmother meant because the older woman pulled away and marched toward the parlor.

"Eli, Mary Grace, I'm staying here and I'll be fine. Let me introduce my friends before you leave."

"Eli" looked none too happy as he motioned Mary Grace to precede him into the room. They both came to a dead stop once over the threshold and Gram chuckled as they surveyed the room full of Gram's bridge partners.

Three older ladies sitting at the bridge table each had a pink lipstick stun gun, the lid off, ready to use, placed within easy reach. Mary Grace recognized the stun guns because she had bought her grandmother one the previous Christmas. Gram must have ordered them for all her friends. The scene didn't surprise her at all. Every good Southern father taught his daughters how to protect themselves from an early age.

They all murmured the appropriate greetings. Mary Grace introduced Ned as her friend and then backed out of the room as fast as possible. Gram followed them to the door.

"So you see, I'll be fine here at Hubert House." Her chin lifted and her eyes turned to steel. Ned took a step back. "In the past, Hubert women have weathered far worse than a few thugs who think they can run over an old woman." She gave a short nod to Mary Grace and spoke with intelligence that showed the sharpness of her mind. "Your old swamp boots are in the shed out back. I assume that's where you're headed. Let me know when you find Bobby. I need to have a talk with that boy. He's always getting into all sorts of trouble. And I expect you to be back in time for Christmas."

Mary Grace grabbed her grandmother in another fierce hug. "Thanks, Gram. We'll be careful and I'll find Bobby. Please take care of yourself. I couldn't stand it if anything happened to you."

They headed out the door, but Ned surprised Mary Grace by turning back. "Ma'am?"

"Yes?" her grandmother answered with patience and graciousness.

"Out of curiosity, why did you choose to call me Eli instead of Nolan?"

Gram had a sparkle in her eye. "Why, didn't you know? In the Bible, Eli was the high priest of Shiloh, the second-to-last Israelite judge succeeded by Samuel."

Ned paused a moment, as if pondering her answer, then moved to leave, determination in his stride. Mary Grace followed him with an equally determined stride. They had a killer to catch before anyone else got hurt, and that included her feisty, adorable grandmother.

TEN

Rounding the corner of the house after helping Mary Grace grab her gear out of the small storage building, Ned heard Krieger barking furiously from inside the car. He took hold of Mary Grace's arm and used the house as cover when she tried to run toward the vehicle.

"Get inside and take care of your grandmother and her friends. Go in the back way. Now!" Her eyes held terror and his heart pounded in his chest. He wouldn't allow anything to happen to this feisty woman who loved Christmas, her rat dog and her sweet grandmother.

His eyes on their car, he spotted movement behind the bumper.

"Go now," he said quietly.

To his relief, she tore off back the way they had come from and Ned pulled his pistol from the waistband of his jeans. When he glanced around the corner of the house, a guy was crawling out from beneath the car. Ned lifted his gun and moved into the open when the guy stood up. "Don't move or I'll shoot," he shouted in warning. The guy had a ball cap pulled low over his brow and Ned failed to get a good look at him. The man stood frozen for a moment, then glanced toward the house with surprise written on his face.

Ned's heart almost pounded out of his chest when a loud rifle report sounded from the front porch and vibrated in the still air. He almost had a heart attack when he heard Mary Grace's voice.

"You leave my dog and my grandmother alone or the next bullet is gonna make you limp for life."

The guy ran off and darted into the woods farther down the driveway. It took everything Ned had not to go after him, but he didn't dare leave Mary Grace alone. The guy might have a partner somewhere close by.

Shoving the pistol back into his jeans, he took several long strides toward the car. He opened the car door and released Krieger. "Krieger, search." Crawling underneath the vehicle, he spotted a simple bomb attached to the car. With steady hands, he examined the device, then carefully pulled a wire free to disable it before removing it from the vehicle. He slid out from under the car, stood and took a deep breath of relief.

He jogged to the front porch, gently pried the shotgun from Mary Grace's fingers and herded her inside. His anger at the risk she'd taken softened at the deep fear reflected in her eyes.

"Everything's okay, but we really need to convince your grandmother to stay somewhere safe. The guy planted a bomb underneath the car."

Gram Ramsey stepped into the foyer and smiled at Ned. "Don't worry, Eli, I'll be safe here. You two go on and find Bobby. I'll be praying for your safety." Her eyes hardened. "And take care of my girl."

He opened his mouth to argue, but she had already

turned to go back and join her bridge partners. Ned could hear the nervous twitters coming from the other ladies over the recent excitement.

Mary Grace gave him a weak smile. "You heard the lady."

There was nothing else to be done, so he opened the door and there sat Krieger in his all-clear position.

"Okay, let's go to the swamp shack and get this thing done."

They got in the car and Mary Grace sat there for a few minutes, worry written on her face. "I couldn't live with myself if something happened to Gram."

Ned started the car. "We'll check out the swamp shack and get back as soon as we can."

"Well," she said with a nervous laugh, "at least now I know your name."

Ned breathed a sigh of relief. He disliked bursting her bubble, but after what had just happened, maybe a different subject would snap her out of her worry over her grandmother. "Your grandmother reminds me of my grandfather and I've found it's just better, in the long run, to go ahead and answer their questions. But I'm afraid you won't find any information on me if you go looking. I don't exist."

She shrugged, when he really wanted her to dig into him. "I get it. You don't trust me, and I'll never know who you really are. Fine, let's just find Bobby. I'll prove he's innocent and you can crawl back to your lonely mountain and I'll be out of your hair for good."

His chest, close to the region of his heart, rejected the idea that he'd never see Mary Grace again. The woman talked too much and poked around in places better left alone, but for some strange reason he wanted her to stay around. He started the car and berated himself. He couldn't afford to trust anyone outside of the chosen few. His and Finn's lives might depend on it.

Back to the task at hand. "Where to?" His flat question had her stiffening in her seat and that was just as well. He had no business becoming attracted to a woman he didn't trust. He couldn't allow himself to forget that she had shown up on his mountain—a place few people even knew existed—to ask for help concerning her brother. A man who had conveniently gone off the grid.

He stopped at the end of the driveway and waited patiently.

She glared at him and motioned to the right. "Go up the road for a mile and we'll park the car in the Okefenokee Swamp public parking lot. Most of the time Bobby and I trekked to the old swamp shack from the back of Gram's house, but sometimes we went in this way because it's easier."

He swiftly turned the wheel and started driving. Within minutes a large wooden sign with some kind of cypress tree carved into it on the left announced the entrance to Okefenokee Swamp Park. A huge red bow was pinned to the top. He turned in and parked the car between two large campers.

Mary Grace opened her door and grabbed the muck boots she'd retrieved from the shack behind her grandmother's house. Using her open door to steady herself, she shed her shoes and pulled the boots on. TB had jumped into the front seat and Mary Grace slipped the dog carrier over her shoulders, stuffed the tiny mutt inside and grabbed her backpack.

Krieger whined from the back seat and Ned felt as if he were living in the twilight zone. His fiercely trained German shepherd had never whined in his life. After slipping on a jacket, she leaned into the car, her fighting face back in place.

"Okay, Mountain Man, let's see how you fare in a swamp. You'll need a jacket. It might be December, but we're in Georgia so you don't have to worry about getting frost bitten like you do on that mountain of yours."

He folded himself out of the car, slipped on a pair of well-worn hiking boots and grabbed his duffel. He shrugged into a light jacket, even though it was hovering around fifty degrees. Compared to Jackson Hole, this felt like springtime. The jacket was mainly to conceal the pistol in the waistband of his jeans. The gun wasn't only because their lives were in danger. He'd been in swamps more times than he cared to remember, places that housed far worse things than a Georgia swamp could ever dream of, but there was still plenty of danger in any swamp. He called Krieger to his side and met Mary Grace at the back of the car. She gave him a haughty stare.

"Dogs are supposed to be on a leash if they aren't being carried."

"Says Miss Rule-Stickler," he mumbled.

"What did you say?"

"Nothing." He shook his head and swept his hand in front of her. "I can control my dog off-leash. Lead the way."

The Georgia princess sniffed and started walking toward an area marked as the park entrance to the swamp. They followed a short path, then stepped onto a planked walkway with a small cable strung through square wood that disappeared into the murky depths of the water.

Mary Grace spoke over her shoulder. "We'll stay on the designated path for about half a mile, and if the old canoe Bobby and I sometimes used when we entered the swamp from this direction is still there and floatable, we can be at the shack fairly quickly."

Ned stared at the lowering sun. "It better be fast or we'll get caught in the swamp after dark."

Mary Grace threw him a challenging grin. "You afraid of a few swamp critters, Ned?"

He gave a mock shudder. "Aye, I'm a mountain man, not a swamp rat like you." He knew how to survive in a swamp, but his words were still true. He much preferred mountain lions and bears to gators.

She marched ahead and soon they stepped off the planked walkway and onto a path. Mary Grace led him into the woods off the designated public pathway and shortly after that they arrived at a slight embankment shouldering a wide expanse of murky water. She muttered under her breath while she searched an area next to a cypress tree, very close to the swamp. The woman never stopped talking. Ned kept a close eye out for gators. They were known to hide right below the surface and strike hard and fast.

Ripping away some undergrowth, she whipped around and pumped a fist in the air. "It's still here, after all this time. If it's floatable, we're in business. If Bobby is at the shack, he had to have gone in from the back of Gram's house."

Ned put Krieger in a Stay and helped her pull the canoe from the clutches of the forest. Green, peeling paint adorned the outside, and it looked water worthy, but Ned pulled it to the edge of the bank and pushed it in to make sure. He let it float a few minutes and, when it didn't take on water, deemed it safe.

They climbed aboard and he grabbed the only set of oars. Mary Grace raised a questioning brow, but he only grunted and started rowing. He had always appreciated nature and found a small measure of peace among the huge cypress trees flourishing in the swamp. Lily pads floated aimlessly in the water and plant life was abundant.

"How far?"

Holding on to both sides of the canoe, she twisted around. "Such a conversationalist. Do you just sit there and grunt when you're on a date?"

Since he hadn't been on a real date in years, he only grunted again.

"It'll only take about ten minutes in the canoe. It's pretty far from civilization. Even if whoever is after us and Bobby found out about this place, it's doubtful they'd ever be able to locate it."

Mary Grace was still twisted toward him in the canoe when Ned saw TB stick her head out of the pouch and her ears prick. He followed the dog's gaze, but before he could make a move or say anything, the rat dog popped out of the pouch, landed on Mary Grace's leg and dove into the water. TB evidently spotted movement and decided a chase was on. Her dog definitely wasn't swamp savvy. As Mary Grace stood screaming in the canoe, threatening to overturn them, Ned muttered out loud,

"Not again," right before he told his dog to stay, slid out of the canoe and prepared to fight a gator. He was right, the woman and her rat dog were nothing but trouble, he thought as he pulled the sharp blade from his boot and placed himself between a hungry gator and his next meal.

Horrified at the scene playing out in front of her, Mary Grace stood frozen in the canoe until Krieger's half growl, half whine broke her trance. She quickly plopped back down, but found herself unable to tear her gaze away. A huge alligator with beady eyes was silently gliding through the water toward Ned. He pushed Tinker Bell toward the canoe.

"Grab your dog out of the water if you can."

His calm words broke through her haze and she went into action, frantically calling Tinker Bell toward the canoe. She recognized the moment her dog realized she was in a precarious position and started paddling her tiny legs as fast as she could. Mary Grace scooped her out of the swamp water, hugged her precious baby close before placing her in the dog carrier, then yelled at Ned, "I have her. Get back in the canoe."

She thought she heard the words *too late now* right before the gator's large mouth yawned wide open in preparation for an attack. Ned dodged the powerful jaws after they snapped shut and grabbed the beast around the mouth, preventing it from attacking again. The water was chest high on Ned, but it looked like he'd found his footing. Her heart in her throat, she sat, mesmerized, as he pulled the gator through the tall grass and onto the embankment. With quick, efficient movements, he released the animal and jumped out of the way. She could now see it was a young alligator as it slithered back into the water, evidently deciding to search for a less troublesome snack elsewhere. It didn't look nearly as dangerous as it had in the water and her breath left her lungs in a giant whoosh when she realized Ned wasn't hurt.

Dripping wet, with his big hands propped on his hips, he stared at her sitting in the canoe. "Now I see why the park requires dog leashes."

She ignored his taunt, so happy no one was hurt, and grabbed the oars, paddling as hard as she could to get to the embankment. She made sure the young gator was long gone before pulling the canoe on land and lifting Tinker Bell from the carrier and placing her on the ground, then racing toward Ned. She reached up high, grabbed his head, pulled it down and planted a big kiss right on his lips.

"I'm so, so sorry. I never dreamed Tinker Bell would jump into the water. I can't believe you risked your life to save her from an alligator. You're a hero, that's what you—"

Her words stopped abruptly when he wrapped his long arms around her waist, lifted her off her feet and kissed her into silence. Only after he dropped her back down did she come to her senses. It took her a moment to assimilate what had just happened. They'd kissed each other, and she liked it. A lot. But that wasn't possible. She knew next to nothing about the man's personal life, and he thought her brother had betrayed him.

"Let it go, Mary Grace. It was only a spur-of-the-moment thing. I can see your thoughts running a mile a minute through that pretty head of yours. It was only a kiss. We need to find the shack and get out of this swamp before dark."

He thought she was pretty? She shook off the fanciful thought. He was right. It was only a we-made-it-through-that-terrifying-ordeal kiss, and she needed to find her brother. After that they would part ways. If the idea left her feeling more than a tad gloomy, she ignored the emotion as she scooped up her dog and climbed back into the canoe. Krieger followed Mary Grace and Tinker Bell. Ned pushed them off and climbed aboard. He rowed and she forced her racing thoughts to silence. All that mattered was finding her brother alive and getting answers. She wouldn't allow anything else to get in the way of that.

As they approached the tree with an upside-down sign reading Mirror Lake that appeared upright in the water's reflection, she motioned for Ned to pull over. She was surprised to see someone had attached a tattered Christmas bow below the sign. Ned hopped out and pulled the canoe onto the bank. Mary Grace stepped out, followed by Krieger, and led them into the wilds of the Okefenokee Swamp. Ned told her to be as silent as possible and let him approach the shack first in case someone had gotten there ahead of them.

On foot it took them fifteen minutes and she breathed a sigh of relief when she spotted the rusted tin roof of the shack. A good portion of the small structure had been taken over by undergrowth. If possible, it looked even worse than it had when she and Bobby used to play there as kids. Gram Ramsey never worried about them in the swamp. She taught them about snakes and alligators and how to avoid them.

Silent as a gentle breeze, Ned gave Krieger a hand

signal that she assumed meant to stay put. Ned slipped past her and moved into the woods to her right. Mary Grace remained hidden behind a huge tree and jerked in surprise when Ned silently appeared on her left. She hadn't even heard him. He must have been really good at his job when he was in the military.

He whispered into her ear, "Looks clear now, but someone has been here." She stiffened and he added, "But I think they're long gone."

She whispered back, "How can you be sure?"

"I found tracks leading to and from the shack, in the opposite direction of the lake."

Mary Grace whipped around in horror. The tracks were from the direction of Gram's house. She closed her eyes and prayed out loud. At the moment she didn't care whether Ned believed or not. "Dear Lord, please, please protect my grandmother."

After a few more seconds, she opened her eyes and leveled a stare at him. "We have to leave right now. What if those prints belong to the bad guys and not Bobby? I can't take that chance because whoever is after us might be headed back to Gram's."

Ned placed his large hands on her shoulders, ignored Tinker Bell's warning growl and looked her in the eye. "Listen, the footprints could belong to your brother. Maybe he holed up here for a while and then left. We're here, so let's check out the cabin and see what we can find."

Mary Grace said another quick prayer and swallowed hard. "Fine. But then we're heading back to Gram's as fast as possible."

He whispered a command to Krieger and the big German shepherd crept through the woods, then reappeared close to the sagging front porch of the shack. The dog slipped inside, and a minute later came back to the front porch and sat.

"All clear, let's go," Ned said.

Mary Grace sent up yet another prayer, asking for direction and information. She hoped Bobby had left a message of some sort and she knew exactly where he would hide it.

Memories assailed her as she stepped through a front door that was barely hanging on by one hinge. It was a one-room shack. No bathroom, no kitchen, only the old table and two chairs she and Bobby had placed there. Her nose wrinkled in distaste. Over the years an entire host of animals had taken refuge in the shack. There were animal droppings everywhere and one corner held a little skeleton, no doubt another animal's dinner.

After prowling the small space, Ned approached the table and picked up an envelope. "It's addressed to you," he said, before tearing the letter open.

"You're rude, you know that?"

"Many people have told me that over the years."

While he studied the letter, Mary Grace casually roamed the room. Precious childhood memories assailed her, but she chided herself to stay focused. With her back to Ned, she quietly pulled the end of a rotten board from the wall and slipped her hand inside. Her heart beat rapidly as her fingers touched something solid. An envelope. One meant for her eyes only.

Mary Grace and Bobby had concealed childhood treasures in their secret hiding place all those years ago in case anyone else visited the swamp cabin, and now she thanked their ingenuity.

Slipping the letter into her jacket pocket, she lightly pushed the board back into place and slowly turned when Ned started talking, his eyes focused on the letter in his hand.

"Your brother is implicating a very powerful person."

Mary Grace rushed to Ned's side, her investigator's nose twitching up a storm. "What does it say?" She grabbed the letter out of his hand, quickly skimming Bobby's words. She went into journalistic overload when his accusations settled into her mind. If what Bobby was saying were true, and she had no reason to doubt him, she was looking at the story of the year. A possible Pulitzer Prize winner.

Her pulse quickened and she looked at Ned. "I can't believe it. Bobby is pointing a finger at Chief of Staff Hensley. He thinks someone overrode his computer the night you and Finn were in that gallery. Ned, he didn't know someone was there waiting for you. This proves he's innocent."

Mary Grace was so filled with joy at proving her brother's innocence she grabbed Ned and gave him a big hug. Mortified to the tips of her toes, she pulled back, but at the same moment, on the fringes of her mind, she heard a noise very similar to the one at Ned's mountain cabin. In a split second, she found herself hefted into Ned's arms while he speared them toward the open front door. Just as they reached the edge of the porch, an ear-splitting explosion rocked the foundation of the shack and the powerful force lifted them into the air.

ELEVEN

Ned twisted his body midair so he would take the full impact of the landing. His breath whooshed from his chest and out of his mouth. He'd have a few bruises on his back, but overall he was convinced they had fared pretty well. The warmth of Mary Grace's body in his arms diverted his attention from their dangerous circumstances. He had grabbed her from behind in the cabin and her soft back was snuggled close to his chest. For a mere moment he allowed himself to consider how different things would be if he could allow himself to trust someone. Mary Grace, with her smart mouth and incessant talk, could easily slip past the protective barriers he'd painfully erected over time.

With years of practice, he compartmentalized any tender emotions and gave a sharp whistle for Krieger, hoping his faithful companion had been outside during the blast. He scrambled up from the ground, placed Mary Grace on her feet, grabbed her hand and guided her toward the nearest trees, keeping them both low. Tree bark stung his face as a bullet hit a tree nearby. It was close, way too close for comfort. Pulling Mary Grace in a zigzag pattern through the woods, he finally got them to the canoe. She clamored aboard and Krieger came tearing behind them and jumped into the craft. Ned pushed them away from the bank as fast as possible and started paddling with all his strength. Thankfully, there was a bend in the river and they lost the shooter. At least for the time being. She was most likely in shock, but he was thankful Mary Grace stayed quiet while he placed some distance between them and the shooter. It was going on full dark now and the enemy could be anywhere, but the darkness was to their advantage.

Mary Grace finally came alive and Ned was glad to see it. Her voice trembled, but he was proud that she was trying to be brave. "What are you doing? Where are we going?"

"Right now I'm putting some distance between us and the shooter. My gut tells me he, or they, will come after us. A swamp is a great place to leave dead bodies. Nobody around to witness the killing, and the swamp critters would most likely take care of the carcasses."

She grimaced, and he almost regretted his words, but he wanted her to realize the extent of the danger they were in.

She slumped her shoulders. "I can't believe someone tried to blow us up again. This is crazy. You'd think someone as powerful as Chief of Staff Hensley could come up with a more inventive way to get rid of us. I can see why someone is trying to kill you, but why me and Bobby?"

Ned had been thinking about that and there was only one reason why they would want Mary Grace dead. "Your brother is up to his eyeballs in this and you're a reporter. Maybe they're afraid Bobby told you something, which he did—he sent you to me—and they know you'll never give up on a juicy story." His last words were filled with sarcasm, but that's how he felt.

Ned kept rowing with quiet efficiency and waited for the storm but was surprised at her insight when she finally spoke.

"Ned, what if they set up Bobby to take the fall, knowing he would run and then contact me? Maybe they were aware Bobby knew where you were and was hoping I would lead them to you."

Ned didn't answer. Night had fallen and the moon was hidden behind a host of clouds. Creatures of the night were awakening with a loud ruckus and Ned had no doubt that there were many gators gliding silently through the swamp, hunting for their next meal.

"We can talk after we set up camp."

"What?" she shrilled.

He grinned when Mary Grace reacted just as he had thought she would. He loved her feistiness. Most women would be in a complete panic after everything that had happened.

"We can't spend the night in the swamp," she insisted. "It's too dangerous and I'm not spending the night alone with you."

"Unless you want to announce our position to the enemy, I suggest you keep your voice down."

Her voice lowered to a furious whisper. "I have to check on Gram. What if someone tries to hurt her. I'd never forgive myself."

Ned knew he had to allay her fears. He loved his grouchy grandfather as much as she appeared to love her gram.

"We'll get there as soon as we can, but it's not safe to travel through the swamp right now. The shooters are probably still out here, and there's always the danger of the swamp critters. We'll wait until daylight before we try to make our way back."

Mary Grace faced forward in the canoe and he heard soft murmurings as she soothed TB. He hadn't thought about how upset the tiny dog would be. Krieger was military trained and gunshots and bombs didn't bother him. It was shocking how drastically Ned's life had changed in such a short period of time. He'd gone from hunting his enemy to protecting a spirited woman and her puff dog.

He steered the canoe toward one of the few solid-looking banks and hopped out, pulling it onto land. Krieger leaped out and Ned held out a hand to Mary Grace. A flash of annoyance crossed her face, but it was accompanied by the barest spark of vulnerability visible in her eyes before she pulled herself together and took his hand.

"Fine, I'll find us a safe spot to sleep," she said quietly. "We probably shouldn't build a fire in case they were able to follow us. At least we didn't take our backpacks off at the cabin. We'll be fine."

It sounded as if she were trying to convince herself, so Ned kept his mouth shut and went about preparing for a night in the swamp. He gathered the largest tree limbs littering the ground and formed them in a circle.

Mary Grace started chattering softly and Ned allowed the soothing cadence of her voice to wash over him. For some unknown reason, her incessant speech was having the oddest effect on him. Instead of getting on his nerves like it had at his cabin, her voice reached a place deep inside him. A place he had closed off long ago, even from his family.

"Ned." She kept her voice at a whisper. "Did you know we only have access to the Okefenokee Swamp today because in the 1800s loggers tried to drain the swamp so they could cut the huge cypress trees?" She chuckled and his heart warmed. "It didn't work, but they did create eleven and a half miles of canals before they were stopped. The canals have been expanded to one hundred and twenty miles."

He took note of the slight tremor in her voice and his respect for her courage slid straight to his heart and sidled up against the warmth he'd received earlier.

She stopped talking, propped her hands on her hips and glared at him. "What, exactly, are you doing?"

He left a small opening at the front of his hastily built fortress and motioned her forward. "This is to keep the gators at bay, at least long enough for us to protect ourselves if they breach the walls. A raised platform would have been better, but this is all we have available."

A myriad of emotions crossed her face and he could almost read her thoughts, she was so transparent. He knew the second she figured it out. Her nose scrunched up and she marched straight up to him. TB popped out of her pouch but ducked back in quickly when she caught sight of Mary Grace's angry expression.

"You lied to me," she whispered fiercely. "You do know how to navigate a swamp."

He grudgingly gave her points for standing up to him, but she wasn't as innocent as she was pretending to be. She had secretly slipped something into her jacket pocket when they were at the shack, and she had yet to share what it was with him.

"You're right, I've fought in much worse swamps than this, but my intent was not to deceive. It was more in jest." He gazed deeply into her eyes, his heart pleading with her to be honest with him. With every fiber of his being, he wanted to be able to trust her.

Casually, he asked, "Have you ever lied by omission, Mary Grace? Have you been completely honest with me?" He held his breath as he waited to see if she would come clean with him.

Mary Grace's heart began to beat triple time. Had Ned seen her slip Bobby's letter into her pocket? No, it was impossible. He'd had his back to her in the shack, reading the letter Bobby left on the table. She gazed into Ned's contemplative eyes. He looked as if he were waiting for her to make a momentous decision and a quick jab punched her gut. This felt like one of those odd turning points in one's life. A moment that could never be taken back or replayed over.

She found herself wanting to slip her hand into her pocket and share the letter with Ned. She believed with all her heart in Bobby's innocence, but what if Bobby had written something private that might appear incriminating to Ned? Ned had promised to bring the full force of the law down on Bobby if he proved his guilt. She couldn't take that chance. She wanted to read the letter so badly, she was burning with curiosity, but she'd have to wait until she had some privacy.

"I appreciate your little joke, but it's time to stop playing games. Now that Bobby has named one of the players in this mess, we have to plan our next move so we'll be ready when we leave the swamp."

She looked away and swallowed hard when something akin to regret and disappointment filled his eyes. Realization dawned like a light butterfly flittering around her heart that she really did care what this few-worded mountain man thought of her. He was slowly penetrating past the heartache of her dysfunctional youth and failed relationships. Almost of its own accord, her hand slowly moved toward her pocket, then fell away.

He gazed at her for a long tense moment, then gestured toward their makeshift fortress. "Let's settle in and we'll make our plans for tomorrow."

Mary Grace scuttled into their small fortress and lay down on the pile of leaves Ned had gathered. Sliding her backpack to the ground, she lay on her back, lifted Tinker Bell from her pouch and pulled a doggy snack from a zippered side compartment. Her dog accepted the treat with the delicacy of a true lady. Krieger bounded inside their temporary home and sat at her feet, a mournful look in his eyes as he gazed adoringly at Tinker Bell. Mary Grace sighed wistfully, half wishing Ned would look at her like that. It wasn't his looks that made her wish for the impossible—although the clean-shaven mountain man was much too handsome for his own good—it was the way he had treated her grandmother. With respect and reverence for her years of wisdom. Pulling out another snack, she offered it to Krieger and was surprised when the dog didn't take the food.

Ned stepped through the opening and gave a curt command. "Okay."

Much to Mary Grace's amazement, the dog gently took the treat from her hand and lay down, eating it slowly, as if the dog biscuit would have to last him a long time.

Mary Grace gave Ned a questioning glance and he shrugged.

"In the past, we've been in situations when we had to go without for days at a time. He's learned to savor it when it's easily won. Most of the time he has to work for it."

Ned got comfortable on the bed of leaves and Mary Grace did the same. She turned her head and stared into the heavens, thinking about what he had said.

"Ned, you have as many layers as a good Southern woman."

"Excuse me?" His startled statement made her smile.

"Just what I said. You're a man of many layers and you have a trunk full of secrets. Southern women are like that. We have our own language and codes."

He snorted and Mary Grace smiled wider, then went digging. "So, do you have any siblings besides your sister?" He stayed quiet so long she didn't think he was going to answer.

He kept his voice in a low whisper. "I have a brother and a sister."

"Will you see them at Christmas? It's only a week away, you know."

She held her breath, waiting to see how much he would reveal. He stayed so still she turned her head to look at him, but it was so dark she couldn't make out his expression.

"I haven't seen my brother in a while. It might be time to go back home."

Mary Grace heard a world of weariness in his voice and she wondered if he was close to his siblings. She knew he loved his niece, but that might not extend to other family members.

Dead leaves rustled and crackled as he shifted position. "Go to sleep. We'll check on your grandmother in the morning, get something to eat, then head to Washington."

So much for sharing personal information. Mary Grace stared into the inky darkness and pondered the future. Was Bobby safe? Was Gram okay? Would she and Ned make it out of the swamp alive? She closed her eyes and prayed that everyone she loved would be safe and they would all be together for Christmas.

"Don't worry, go to sleep. I'll keep watch for both human and animal predators. Your thoughts are almost as loud as when you're talking."

His disgruntled words had her smiling again. "Don't worry, Mountain Man, I'll say a prayer for you, too."

They quit whispering and the night creatures of the swamp were a comfort in one sense, due to growing up in Georgia, but she wouldn't have allowed herself to drift off if Ned hadn't been there. She knew he'd protect her, and in her sleepy haze, she realized she trusted him to watch over her. Tinker Bell snuggled against her chest and Mary Grace curled onto her side, almost asleep when Krieger, who was lying across the entrance of their mini-walled shelter, released a low, vicious growl.

TWELVE

Ned winced when Mary Grace sat upright and whispered loudly enough to draw anyone hunting them to their location. "What is it? Is something out there? Ned! Do you hear me?"

It was so dark beneath all the cypress trees loaded with hanging moss, he could barely see her pale face. Instead of answering, he reached out and laid a hand on her shoulder. Leaning in close, he whispered in her ear, "It's probably a wild animal. I'll check the perimeter. It'll only take a few minutes."

But it wasn't an animal. Krieger had been trained and the growl he released portended trouble, of the human kind. Ned admired her quick assessment of the situation when she grabbed his hand on her shoulder and squeezed it tight, lowering her voice even more.

"We can't stay here. You would have left the swamp earlier, but I know you were worried about my safety, so you chose to spend the night. I don't know if the person who blew up the shack and shot at us has found us, but we're sitting ducks. It's been a long time, but I know this swamp pretty well. I can get us out of here. I know several shortcuts to Gram's, but we'll have to go slowly and watch out for sinkholes." Ned could barely make out her anticipating grin. "If whoever is after us gets caught in the swamp mud, they'll have to remove their boots to get out and that'll slow them down."

Ned assessed her hasty plan. A swamp was dangerous at night, which is why he had decided to stay put with a woman and fluff dog in tow, but a swamp in Georgia was far different than some of the places he had fought while in the military.

"Can't you at least trust me on this?" she hissed quietly.

The annoyance in her voice made him smile— something he'd done more of since meeting Mary Grace than he had in a long time. He knew the heavy guilt he carried over Finn had pretty much taken over his life, but he was so close to finding the culprit, or culprits, he could almost smell it. But to answer Mary Grace's question. Did he trust her? She still hadn't told him what she'd found in the shack. But in the end, did it matter? After this was over, they would go their separate ways.

"Maybe." He grunted when a sharp elbow jabbed him in the side. Not many people would've had the courage to do what she had just done, much less argue with or tease him. And that included his own family, at least since the incident with Finn.

"Just for that I might let you fall into a bog and leave you there."

"You wouldn't do that," he surprised himself by saying.

She sniffed. "Well, at least you trust me that much. Let's grab our gear and go."

"Let's get out of here," he agreed.

"Fine by me. I'll lead the way. Stay close. I have a flashlight in my backpack, but I won't turn it on until we reach the dangerous places. We're taking the short-cut to Gram's."

She stuffed the mutt back inside the dog carrier, then tugged on his sleeve. He and Krieger allowed her to lead the way. He had no problem allowing a person, man or woman, to take charge of a situation if they were more knowledgeable about the current circumstances. Hyperalert, Ned scanned the area as they moved quietly through the swamp. They were heading away from Mirror Lake at a fairly rapid pace, but they didn't get far before Krieger released another low growl, indicating someone was right on their heels.

Mary Grace must have understood what was going on. She dropped back a couple of steps and whispered in his ear, "I have a plan. Stay right behind me and try to step exactly where I do." Ned's instinct was to circle around and surprise their company from behind, but he couldn't risk leaving Mary Grace.

"Lead on," Ned said, surprising himself. Mary Grace might know the swamp, but Ned was an expert at guerrilla warfare. If he were still a praying man, he would have asked for help, but the Almighty hadn't seen fit to help Finn and Ned's faith had taken a nosedive. He'd learned to take care of himself just fine.

Ned gave a hand signal to Krieger and the dog followed him closely from behind. He did his best to step where she did, but it was hard to see. It had gotten even darker the farther they traveled into the swamp. She slowed to a stop in front of him and he placed his lips close to her ear.

"Why did we stop?"

"Shh, wait and listen. Just give it a moment. I want to make sure my trap worked, then we'll move on."

Ned stood behind her, not moving a muscle. He could stay motionless for hours if need be. He'd done it plenty of times in the past, but he almost failed to hear the quiet commotion behind them because the cinnamon smell in her hair had assailed his senses. The woman was a walking Christmas card, ugly sweaters and all.

The night creatures suddenly went still and frantic whispers floated through the air.

"I need help. I'm buried in the mud up to my calves," one guy hissed.

"I'm in the same situation," a calm, authoritative voice answered. "We'll have to leave our boots behind. Lift one leg out slowly and try to find firm ground, but make it fast."

"Why?" the first guy asked, a slight tremor in his voice.

"Because there's a gator headed our way and I don't plan on being his next meal."

The first guy gave up all pretense of keeping their location a secret and belted out, "This is not what I signed up for. I was only supposed to accompany you. The boss wanted to make sure you did the job right."

Humor laced the second man's voice. "Well, now, if you make it out of the swamp alive, you can report everything to your boss."

Ned heard a pft, pft, double rapid suppressed fire, and knew some gator had probably met his death. Either that or the professional hit man had just rid himself of his employer's tattletale appendage.

Ned nudged Mary Grace forward. He didn't have time to round up the two men behind him for questioning. His first priority was to get Mary Grace to safety.

After hearing the muffled report of the gunshots, Mary Grace stumbled forward when Ned nudged her from behind. As a reporter, she'd been in some dicey situations in her life, but nothing compared to this. She prayed the man with the calm, icy-sounding voice had shot a gator instead of the whiny man accompanying him. She had known they were in danger, but actually hearing the two men in the swamp somehow made it much more real. And personal. Very personal.

She led the way out of the swamp, but with every step she took, anger replaced her initial fear. How dare someone set up her brother and try to kill her, Bobby and Ned. She became very determined to expose everyone involved in this mess. And at Christmas, of all times. It was the birth of Christ, a time for people to come together with good cheer.

About thirty minutes later, she stepped into the clearing at the back of Gram's property, but Ned grasped her arm.

"Let me check the area, see if anyone is watching the house."

She nodded her assent and sighed when he commanded Krieger to stay with her and Tinker Bell. Ned always seemed to protect everyone in his care, but she briefly wondered if anyone protected him. Was he close to his family, or had the mission with Finn changed him? She jumped when he soundlessly appeared at her side.

"Stop doing that," she whispered jerkily.

"Doing what?" he asked, all innocence.

She ignored his taunt. "Can we approach the house? I want to check on Gram."

"We're clear. I'm sure your grandmother is okay, but I don't want to take any chances that someone else might be in there. Do you have a key? I can jimmy the lock if you don't."

Upon hearing his words, Mary Grace scrambled around the side of the house and up the steps leading to the front porch. Going to the bench swing, she took hold of the left chain connecting the swing to the ceiling and crimped it, pulling the links apart. Ned crowded behind her and watched as she removed a spare key that had been interwoven with the other links.

"Ingenious," he exclaimed as he followed her, breathing down her neck, to the front door.

"Thanks. It was Bobby's idea."

Anxious to make sure Gram was safe, she turned the key in the lock, and wished she hadn't mentioned her brother because she literally felt Ned stiffen behind her. Well, that was too bad. She loved Bobby and had no doubts of his innocence. She would always protect her brother.

She cringed when the lock clicked as she turned the key. The letter from Bobby tucked away in her pocket probably proved his point about the trust issue. She hadn't exactly been honest with him, but she had to read the letter before she'd even think about allowing Ned to see it.

Ned pulled her behind him when she pushed the door inward and slid in front of her, entering the house first. Irritation rippled through her. She was used to taking care of herself, but memories of the sounds of muffled gunfire in the swamp made her shiver. She decided having six and a half feet of muscle go in front of her to make sure the house was safe didn't make her any less independent or strong.

She wanted nothing more than to check on Gram, but she silently followed Ned and Krieger through the downstairs, checking every room. She had to shush Tinker Bell a couple of times. They circled back to the foyer and she pointed toward the beautiful double staircase leading to the second floor. They took the one on the left and slowly made their way up the steps. On the landing, Mary Grace pointed left again and tugged on his shirt when they reached Gram's room. She stepped around Ned, cracked the door open and assured herself that Gram was still safely tucked in. A soft, gentle snore reached her ears and she grinned. Being a gentile Southern woman, Gram would have been horrified if she knew she snored. Mary Grace pulled the door closed.

"I don't want to scare her. There's no one in the house and I'm hungry. Why don't we go downstairs and raid the refrigerator?" She desperately wanted to read the letter from Bobby, but her empty stomach had decided otherwise.

He nodded and they retraced their footsteps to the kitchen. Mary Grace flipped on a light and the two-hundred-year-old patina oak floor shone dully in the reflection. Like everything else in the house, the floor needed resurfacing.

After pulling Tinker Bell out of the dog carrier and placing her on the floor, she immediately went to the pantry and pulled out a small bag of dog food.

"Gram always keeps a bag of food here for Tinker Bell in case we pop in for a visit."

Ned eyed the tiny bag askance, probably thinking Krieger could eat the whole bag in one meal, and Mary Grace giggled, then closed her mouth in horror. She never giggled. She definitely wasn't a woman who giggled. She was a White House press correspondent, not a Georgian debutante, although her grandmother had done her best to turn her into one. She felt her chosen profession was a gift from God. She'd always stood strong for the underdog. She slid a sideways glance at Ned as she took two dog bowls from a lower cabinet. He didn't appear to be an underdog, but she'd do her best to help him find justice. *After* proving her brother was innocent.

She poured food into the bowls and Tinker Bell pounced, but Krieger sat on his haunches, his gaze on Ned and saliva stringing out both sides of his mouth.

"Eat," Ned commanded, and the dog slowly approached the food.

Mary Grace filled the bowl twice more before the dog finished and went to lay down beside his new best friend. Tink growled, but allowed Krieger to snuggle up against her small dog bed.

Opening the refrigerator door, Mary Grace's stomach rumbled and she clapped her hands together when she spotted leftover lasagna. "Yes! We're in business." Pulling out the casserole dish, she made quick work of placing food on two plates and sticking them in the microwave one at a time. The aroma of Gram's homemade meat sauce titillated her nose and she placed both plates on the kitchen island after they heated. Grabbing silverware out of a drawer in the cabinet near the sink, she tore off two paper towels and motioned for Ned to sit. "Dig in while it's hot."

He slid onto the stool beside her and tucked into his food.

Mary Grace spoke between bites. "I can't believe I'm so hungry, but if you think about it, I haven't had anything substantial since before climbing your mountain. I had snacks for Tinker Bell, but only a few energy bars for myself, and those don't really count." She stopped chewing when he just stared at her.

"What? Haven't you ever seen a woman eat before?"

He raised a bushy brow. He might have shaven all that hair off his face, but his brows were still bushy.

"I like a woman with a healthy appetite." He then lowered his fork to his plate, rose and placed the plate in the sink, his broad back to her. "We should get some rest. It's going to be a long day tomorrow."

Her stomach plummeted. In the past, Mary Grace had been accused of acting like a dog with a bone, never giving up until she had ferreted out every tiny piece of information there was to be found on a story, but somehow Ned had become more than a story.

She slid off the bar stool and placed her plate in the sink next to his. They stood shoulder to shoulder, staring out the small window overlooking the side of the house.

"I'm sorry," she said softly, regretting what could never be. "Your private life is none of my business. We'll catch whoever is trying to kill us and then you can go back to your mountain and your privacy."

He moved so fast, she was startled when he turned, wrapped his arms around her waist and pulled her close.

She melted into his arms when his lips gently touched her own. For a man so large and gruff, he was gentle as a lamb. Pulling back, he dropped his forehead against hers, as if deep in thought. She had no idea what was going on in his mind.

She smiled weakly and pulled away, her heart saddened. She could never date a man who was convinced her brother had betrayed him, and then there were the trust issues.

Avoiding his searching gaze, she headed out of the kitchen. "We should get some sleep. There are plenty of bedrooms. You can take your pick."

As soon as she had Ned settled in his room, Mary Grace wearily made her way to her old room. Sitting on the quilt-covered mattress, she snapped on the table lamp and pulled Bobby's letter out of her pocket.

Running her finger along the sealed edge, she pulled the handwritten note from the envelope. She skimmed it once, then slowly read it again and closed her eyes, her heart saddened beyond belief. "Dear Lord, please, I'm asking that You help Ned through this impossible situation." She opened her eyes and read the note a third time. Bobby pretty much repeated the same thing as he did in the letter Ned had read—about Chief of Staff Hensley—but he added one more important, earth-shattering piece of information that Ned didn't know about. If Bobby was right, Ned's world, and faith—if he had any left—was getting ready to be blown to smithereens, right here at Christmas, because Bobby mentioned a second name in her letter: Finn.

THIRTEEN

Throwing his duffel onto the floor next to the bed, Ned pulled out his cell and checked the time. Three a.m. in the States meant it would be eight o'clock in the morning in Scotland. Finn should be awake. Before he made the call, he sat there, weary to the bone while memories assailed him. He'd met Finn in Jackson Hole when his family spent part of the school year in the family home where his sister and niece, Sylvia and Fran, were now temporarily residing. Ned had tutors when they traveled, but his parents wanted him to spend time with other children and made sure they were in Jackson Hole for at least half of the school year.

He and Finn had pretty much grown up together, then they both joined the military and served the country that had been so good to them.

He stared at the phone in his hand and thought about his best friend. The reason Finn always tagged along to Scotland with him was because his childhood family life had been less than ideal. His father drank a lot and there was always dissension and quite a bit of yelling in his household.

With a short sigh, Ned made the call. He'd love a hot bath, but that could wait until morning. Finn answered on the third ring.

"Where have you been? I've been worried sick about you."

"Good morning to you, too."

"I can't believe you're not keeping me in the loop. I should be helping you, not tucked away safely in Scotland where no one can find me."

Ned rubbed his tired eyes with his free hand. "Finn, we've been over this before. I can't be worried about you while I'm trying to find the people responsible for putting you in that wheelchair."

"I'm not helpless, you know."

"I realize that. I can share a few things. I'm with Bobby Lancaster's sister. I'm hoping we'll be able to find Bobby. He's gone off the grid, but we'll catch up to him. Hopefully he'll have some answers."

Ned chose not to tell Finn about the letter Bobby had left at the shack. He didn't want his friend to worry because this thing went to the top in Washington. Ned assured himself Finn was safe in the cottage he had rented for him but cautioned him, nonetheless.

"You're staying out of public view?"

"Yes, Daddy," Finn said snidely, "but I'm going stir crazy. It's time to wrap this up so things can get back to normal."

Ned overlooked Finn's testiness. He'd have been irritated, too, if the situation were reversed.

"Did you get the money I sent?"

"Yes, thanks," he replied grudgingly.

Ned rubbed his forehead. He knew it was hard for

Finn to take money from him, but after he caught their betrayer, Finn could find a job and his ego would be restored. At least Ned hoped that would be the case. Finn had always been good with technology. He shouldn't have a problem finding work.

"So this sister, Mary Grace Ramsey, what's she like?"

Ned stiffened. He was exhausted and just wanted to crawl into bed. He didn't want to discuss Mary Grace, but if it would give Finn something else to think about, he'd share a few details.

Ned smiled for the first time during the call. "The woman's a pistol. She chatters a lot and owns a rat dog named Tinker Bell."

"What does she do for a living?"

Ned gripped the phone harder. This wasn't going to go over well. "She's a reporter, a White House press correspondent."

"What?" Finn practically screamed into the phone. "Ned, you have to dump her. Most of what we do in the CIA is classified. If she finds out about some of the stuff we've done, it'll be all over the news. You can't let that happen."

Ned stiffened again. He was tired and Finn was grating on his nerves. "I'll handle it. You don't need to worry."

Finn paused. "You like her. I can hear it in your voice. Ned, you can't have a relationship with a reporter."

Ned rubbed the bridge of his nose and closed his eyes. "I know. Listen, it's 3:00 a.m. here. I'm going to bed."

"I'm sorry, buddy," Finn said, sounding contrite. "Life sometimes throws us curveballs and we just have to learn to deal with them."

Guilt weighed even heavier on his shoulders. Finn was in that wheelchair because of him and would be for the rest of his life.

"I'm sorry, Finn." He'd apologized a hundred times, but it would never be enough.

"Don't feel sorry for me," Finn snapped. "Just catch these guys so we can move on."

"I'll do my best," Ned said and ended the call.

He had one more uncomfortable phone call to make before he could rest. He needed help and there was one person he trusted more than anyone. He punched in the number and waited. It rang twice.

"Aye," a smooth Scottish burr answered in his ear. The butler's all-too-familiar voice placed a yearning in Ned's heart for the home of his forbearers. Over the years, he'd spent more time in the United States than in Scotland, but his ancestry sometimes called to him, like now, when he was confused and tired. Tired of carrying the guilt over Finn and confused over the woman sleeping several doors away from him.

He stretched out on the bed and grinned. "Aye, Alfred," he said, slipping into his comfortable Scottish burr. It felt right. "'Tis the middle child calling." Alfred had been with the family since Ned's father was young. No one knew exactly how old the man was, but Alfred always knew everything that went on inside Dundar Castle.

"Is Angus taking care of himself?"

Alfred sniffed. "Nay, ye grandfather is a stubborn man. He won't adhere to the special diet the doctor placed upon him for the touch of diabetes he's developed. Would ye like to speak to him? I believe he's breaking his fast."

Ned would love to talk to the old man, but that would have to wait until later. "Nay, let him eat in peace. I'll speak to Ewan if he's available."

A pause, then, "Aye, he's in the library. I'll get him for ye, and, Ned, it's time for ye to come home."

Ned waited on the line for his brother to answer and smiled, thinking about his grandfather eating breakfast. The old man had probably bribed the kitchen staff to serve him something that would make his doctor scream and yell in frustration. He'd visit the castle when this was over and encourage Angus to eat better. Ned wanted his grandfather to stay healthy for a long time to come.

"Yes?" a curt voice answered.

"Hey, bro, didn't Alfred tell you it was me?"

Ned heard the old office chair creak as Ewan leaned back. The furniture in the castle was almost as old as the castle itself. The place was loaded with antiques and art.

"No, he said it was a surprise. What's wrong?"

That was Ewan, straight to the point. "What? I can't call my brother to say hello?"

"No, not since you decided to carry the weight of the world on those broad shoulders of yours." Ewan paused again. "Listen, Ned, it's not your fault that Finn was injured."

"Stop! I don't need a lecture." He paused and sorted out his thoughts. "I'm close, Ewan. I'm going to catch these guys, but I need a little help. I need use of the political connections you've made through the art gallery and that Machiavellian mind of yours to help me come up with a plan. I heard your last bestseller made quite the stir in Germany."

"It's all fiction, Ned, you know that."

"Aye, if it's fiction, why did the German chancellor lose her position?"

Ewan signed. "Tell me what's going on."

Ned caught him up to speed and they started working on a plan to trap Chief of Staff Hensley. Ned ended the call when Ewan got a little personal, asking questions about Mary Grace.

He lay there a minute, going over both conversations in his mind. Something niggled at the back of his brain, but he was too tired to figure it out. Sitting up, he pulled his boots off and lay back on the bed without even removing his clothes.

Waking up the next morning, the first thing Mary Grace noticed was her dry mouth. She grimaced when she realized she'd been so tired the previous night, she hadn't even brushed her teeth, much less taken a shower. At some point she'd crawled beneath the quilt, but when she tried to move, she found herself completely penned in.

Lifting her head off the pillow, she laughed when she realized Krieger was laying across her legs and Tinker Bell was snuggled against his back. She tried to pull her legs out from under the huge dog, but it was useless until he roused and stood, stretching on all fours. The massive dog padded his way to her head and licked her on the chin. Not to be outdone, Tink barked and scooted up and over Mary Grace's body to take prime position.

Mary Grace loved on both the animals before shoving them aside. "I'll take you both out in a few minutes. Let me at least brush my teeth." She made her way to the bathroom and smothered a scream when she glanced in the mirror. Her hair looked like a rat's nest and she had a huge pillow crease on her cheek. Thankfully Gram had remodeled when they still had a good bit of money and installed private bathrooms in all the bedrooms. Before that, there had been a shared bathroom at the end of both halls that housed the bedrooms. There was no way she wanted Ned to see her like this.

She eyed the shower with acute anticipation, but Tink barked and Mary Grace knew she'd have to let the dogs out first. Maybe Ned was still asleep and wouldn't see her looking so horrible, but then again, what did it matter? Yes, the man had kissed her, but when she shared Bobby's letter, that would never happen again. She was sure of it.

With that depressing thought in mind, her untied robe flapping around her legs, she left her bedroom and trotted down the left stairway with the dogs on her heels. Just as she reached the bottom stair, Ned stepped out of the kitchen with a steaming cup of coffee in his hand. He was clean-shaven, had on jeans and a khaki shirt, and his hair was much shorter than it had been.

She stopped in front of him and scrutinized the new look. It was a little jagged on the ends and Mary Grace grinned. "I see Gram got her scissors out."

He grimaced, then shrugged. "I was due for a trim."

It tickled her how a woman as small as her gram could wield so much authority over such a large man, but then she became aware of the way she looked.

"Yes, well, I have to let the dogs out."

She turned to go, but Ned gently grabbed her elbow. "I'll handle the dogs, go take your shower."

They stood frozen, gazing into one another's eyes. For a moment in time, Mary Grace mourned the loss of what would never be—there was too much standing between them. He was a man full of secrets and she was a journalist—a person who revealed secrets to the world. And most of all, there was Bobby. She doubted Ned would ever fully trust her brother, even after she had proven his innocence.

On her way to her bedroom, she thought about Bobby's letter. She really wanted to show it to Ned—be completely honest with him—but maybe she should do some research first and find out more about the other name listed in her private letter. Even Bobby admitted he could be wrong, which is why he hadn't mentioned Finn in the letter left on the table at the shack.

She knew Ned would never forgive her for not being completely upfront, but if Bobby was wrong, she had a chance to prevent a lot of heartache for Ned. By the time she had whirled into her bedroom, more than ready to grab a shower and wash off the swamp stink from the previous day, she had formed a plan and knew whom she could call for help. A man who'd done work for her in the past.

She almost skidded to a stop when she saw her gram coming out of her bathroom. Dressed in slacks and a silk blouse, with perfect hair and a full face of makeup, her grandmother looked horrified when she lifted her head as Mary Grace stopped in front of her.

"Young lady, I was looking for you. Please tell me you didn't go downstairs without dressing first. Did Eli see you looking like something a stray dog dragged up?"

Mary Grace loved her gram, but the older woman really was steeped in outdated traditions. Then again, Mary Grace's love life was in the pits, so maybe she should listen to her grandmother. Make some changes. It sure couldn't hurt.

She did her best to appear abashed. "Yes, ma'am. The dogs had to use the bathroom. I know that's no excuse, but it's the only one I've got."

Her grandmother smiled and opened her arms. "Come here, baby, give your gram a big hug."

Mary Grace flew into her arms and all the fears and frustrations of the last couple of days came tumbling out. "Oh, Gram, I'm so worried about Bobby, and Ned thinks Bobby may be mixed up in what happened to him and Finn. And Ned kissed me, but it can't come to anything because Ned thinks Bobby is partially responsible for putting Finn in a wheelchair and the whole thing is just awful. There's some powerful politicians involved in this mess and it's dangerous. I really wish you would move in with your friend Sadie until this is over."

Her grandmother pulled back, took her by the arm and they both sat on the edge of the bed.

"Now, let's put things in perspective. I don't know all the details, but we both know Bobby would never do anything immoral. I helped raise that boy and I know he's innocent of whatever Ned thinks he's done." Gram smiled wryly. "But that's not to say Bobby wasn't used in some way without his knowledge. For a genius, the boy doesn't have a lick of common sense when it comes to devious dealings."

Gram rubbed Mary Grace's hair like she used to when she was a kid and it soothed her senses.

"Now, I want to know how you feel about Eli."

Mary Grace swiped the tears from beneath her eyes and smiled sadly. "It doesn't matter how I feel about him. There are too many things keeping us apart and I've known him for less than thirty-six hours. I'll not make the same mistakes my mother made. She rushed into marriage twice and both times were a disaster."

Gram placed both hands on Mary Grace's cheeks. "Sweetheart, I've told you this many times. Your mother has a disease. It's called gambling." She sighed and removed her hands. "I've prayed for her and it's now in God's hands."

She took Mary Grace's hand and held it with both of her own. "My sweet baby girl, you can't let your mother's mistakes rule your life. You have to trust that God knows best. If you do develop feelings for Eli, don't allow your past to ruin it for you."

Mary Grace dropped her head on her grandmother's shoulder. "Thanks, Gram."

Feeling much better, she stood up and grinned, wanting to lighten the mood. "Oh, well, after seeing what I look like in the morning, I probably scared the man off, anyway."

She hugged her gram and headed for the shower. Twenty minutes later, dressed, her hair pulled back in a wet ponytail, she followed the scent of bacon to the kitchen. Her stomach rumbled even though they'd raided the kitchen the night before.

She walked into a picture of domestic bliss, judging by the expressions on Ned's and both the dogs' faces. Mary Grace headed to the coffeepot, poured herself a cup, then leaned her backside against the counter and stared at her grandmother.

"Eggs and ham for the dogs, Gram?"

Sitting across from Ned at the small table placed in front of the bay window, Gram sniffed. "I don't get to see Tinker Bell very often and it's my pleasure to spoil her while she's here."

Mary Grace took that as a subtle reminder that she hadn't visited as often as she should. You had to listen close to Southern women to catch the nuisances of a conversation. She blew on her coffee and took a sip.

"What about Krieger?"

Gram beamed across the table at Ned. "Eli explained that Krieger has faithfully served our country in the past, so he deserves a good hot meal."

Mary Grace was just getting ready to grab a plate when suddenly, without warning, one glass panel of the bay window shattered and a barrage of bullets tore into the wall across the kitchen. Before she could move, Ned had shoved Gram down onto the seat. Krieger started growling fiercely. Shaken to the core, Mary Grace dropped to the floor and crawled toward Gram. Gently taking her arm, she helped the older woman out of the seat and to the floor.

Ned had already ducked under the table and was standing away from the window.

"Take care of your grandmother and stay away from any windows. I'll find the shooter if he decided to hang around." The calm authority mixed with solid fierceness in his voice stilled her trembling. She nodded, and he and Krieger left the room.

Mary Grace pulled her grandmother to a safe area away from the window and helped her to her feet. She hugged her gram fiercely and tears came to her eyes. Pulling back, she peered into brave, wise old eyes. "Gram, please, for my sake, go and stay with one of your friends until this is over." Mary Grace choked on her next words. "I can't stand the thought of something happening to you."

Gram raised a hand and gently wiped away Mary Grace's tears. "My dear child, only God knows when it's my time to go. But for your peace of mind, I'll do as you ask."

Mary Grace hugged her again. "Thanks, Gram. I hope it won't be for long."

The front door opened and closed, and Mary Grace pushed her grandmother behind her, but it was Ned. She sent him a questioning glance and he shook his head.

"Whoever took the shot is long gone. Krieger and I cleared the area. He didn't try again, so I'm assuming he's by himself now and doesn't want to take a chance on getting caught." He looked at Gram. "You alright, ma'am?"

Gram stepped forward and lifted her chin. "I'm fine, Eli. Thank you for asking. I've decided to stay with a friend until this is over. Now, I want your promise that you'll see no harm comes to my granddaughter."

Ned nodded grimly. "Yes, ma'am. I'll do my best."

Fifteen minutes later, after saying a tearful goodbye to her aging grandmother when her friend picked her up, they gathered their stuff to leave.

The letter she'd stuffed back into her pocket was at the forefront of her mind now that Gram was safe. At some point, she'd have to tell Ned what Bobby wrote and it saddened her heart to realize that this may very well be the last time she and Ned would be even somewhat in accord.

FOURTEEN

Overnight one of Ned's contacts had someone pick up the car they'd left in the Okefenokee Swamp parking lot and deliver it to Mary Grace's grandmother's house, so they could make it back to the airstrip without relying on a taxi driver to lose a tail. Now Ned's plane was lifting off, heading to DC.

Suspicious about the item Mary Grace had found in the shack and still hadn't shared with him, Ned waited until she excused herself from the cockpit on the premise of checking her emails. He logged on to the server, hoping to slip into her email through the onboard Wi-Fi, but she was password-protected. He could have hacked in, but his heart wasn't in it.

The conflicting emotions of attraction and mistrust warred constantly with each other, but he had good reason. She'd lied to him by omission and he couldn't live with that. Maybe he should demand to see what she'd found, but another part of him wanted her to trust him enough to volunteer the information.

He shook his head. He never wavered like this. He had been trained to be in control of every possible scenario and situation. His life sometimes depended on it. Gram's words of faith and prayer had hit their mark, but he pushed them aside and concentrated on the task at hand.

Pulling out the satellite phone, he called his brother.

Ewan answered with a clipped, "Yes?" His older brother was fighting his Scottish heritage by not using the brogue he had grown up with. Ewan and their grandfather butted heads all the time and this was Ewan's way of rebelling against the expectation of being named laird of the clan. It amused Ned. In the States the title sounded outdated, but in Scotland it was still very real. Much like the aristocracy in England. Not what it once was, but still there.

"Ewan, it's Ned. We're in the air and I'm on a secure line."

"About time you called. I've been busy."

"Tell me."

"I made a few calls to friends with high connections in Washington who like to chat. I casually dropped the information that you're dating a journalist who is very interested in your and Finn's story. That should be enough to prompt the chief of staff to do something rash and reveal himself."

"Ned, I don't have to remind you that you're playing a very dangerous game. If Hensley is involved, things are going to get very dicey. He won't take this lying down. He'll come after you. Do you trust the information Mary Grace's brother left you?"

Ned gripped the phone hard, but slowly relaxed his fingers. "Not entirely, but it's the only lead I have at the moment and someone is after me, anyway," he said wryly. "I think they want to get rid of any loose ends and Finn and I are loose ends. Mary Grace's brother is a loose end, too, even if he's in it with them."

Mary Grace's laughing golden eyes flashed in his mind. He didn't like that she was in danger, but her brother was responsible for that.

"You told me she got shot on your mountain. I know her brother is involved, but why would they come after her?"

Ewen's question was a good one. "Aye, why would they? Maybe her brother got in too deep and realized the error of his ways. Then he got worried about his sister and sent her to me. I really don't know the answer to your question, yet, but they have to know she's a reporter and they would only use her as a last resort, through her brother, to try to find me since Bobby went off the grid."

The thought didn't sit well with Ned and he was ready to get off the phone.

"Be careful, brother. You do know if anything happens to me, you're next in line for the position of laird." Laughing into the phone, Ewan ended the call.

Ned grinned, despite himself. In the old days, long, long ago, the position of laird would be highly coveted, but in these modern days, no one wanted it. Ned grinned wider, thinking how slick his own father had been. He had removed himself from the role. To keep the old castle and grounds up, he claimed he had to spend his time running the family's art galleries, which was pretty much the truth. The old castle took a lot of money to operate, but it was the family seat and the community also depended on them in a lot of ways.

Staring at the onboard computer, Ned could see that Mary Grace was still online, even though he couldn't see what she was working on. He halfway lifted himself out of his seat, thinking he should demand to see what she had found in the shack, but then he slid back down. He really wanted her to fully trust him and share the information herself.

He gave a gruff snort. He didn't trust her, so how could he expect her to trust him? He'd let it go until they reached Washington, and if she hadn't shared by then, he'd demand to see what she was hiding. He had to have every scrap of information if they were going to beat the sly politicians in Washington. And he had a gut feeling that things were going to move fast as soon as they hit the ground.

His sat phone rang and he answered with a gruff "Aye." Very few people had the number.

"Ned, it's Madeline."

"Ma'am, good to hear from you." That's all he said. As was his customary response, he waited patiently.

She sighed into the phone. "You never were one to chitchat. I take it this is a secure line?"

His lips curled at the edges. "You have to ask?"

She chuckled. "No, but it's always smart to make sure. I wanted to check on you. I was a bit surprised by our last conversation and concerned that you were dealing with a journalist."

Ah, so that's what this was about. "Don't worry, I can handle Mary Grace."

A slight hesitation, then, "Well, that's good to hear."

He waited again.

"Listen, Ned, I know you want justice for what happened to Finn, but what will it gain you? Finn will still be in a wheelchair."

Ned stiffened. Was the CIA director—his boss, or maybe his previous boss if he chose not to return after his leave of absence—warning him off? He trusted her implicitly and she should trust him to handle the situation. "Is there something you're not telling me?"

She quickly backed down. "No, no, you've served your country honorably and I just thought you might want to get on with your life. Is Mary Grace Ramsey still traveling with you?"

Interesting that she'd ask about Mary Grace, but also plausible. He was spending time with a woman who exposed others as a profession.

"She's still with me. We're heading to DC, and let me assure you, you don't have to worry about anything."

She accepted his assurance and ended the call.

Settled on a plush leather seat with the laptop on the tray in front of her, it took quite a while for Mary Grace to read her emails from work.

After she finished, she looked down at both dogs curled on the floor near her feet. They were giving her accusing stares.

"Hey, don't look at me like that. I haven't done anything wrong."

But she felt as if she had. Hiding the letter from Ned was the right thing to do, but she still felt like a heel. She glanced back at the dogs. "Okay, here's the deal. If Bobby is right about Finn, I'll tell Ned immediately, but if he's wrong, Ned won't ever have to know or live through the pain it would cause."

She rolled her eyes. "And why am I sitting here talking to two dogs?"

Pulling up a new draft, she started writing an email to a private investigator she knew. A man she trusted and one who had done a lot of work for her in the past.

She asked him to check into Finn and went for the full service. Background, financials, personal life. The works. She also wanted the information ASAP. She hit Send and it didn't take but a minute or so to get a response: This is gonna cost you.

She smiled and ruefully thought of her bank balance. She made good money, but wouldn't be able to get reimbursed unless she wrote a story connected to the request.

She typed in I know, and hit Send.

Sitting back in her chair, she gazed at both the dogs, thinking for a moment before returning her gaze to the computer. She hunched over the laptop and sent Bobby a fairly inane email, one that wouldn't mean anything to anyone watching the account, but would tell him she was alive and well if he was able to sneak in and check.

She sat back again and pondered everything that had happened. This was the first time since this whole thing began that she'd had time to relax and really process all the events.

In her private letter, Bobby didn't go into detail about how he had gotten involved or set up. She'd have to wait until they found him to get that information.

She laughed when Tinker Bell hopped into her lap and Krieger whined because the love of his life had abandoned him. Mary Grace ran a hand over the silky fur of her dog's back and spoke to the big German shepherd. "Don't worry, Krieger, I'll get Gram to make you a Christmas sweater to match Tinker Bell's."

The image of the proud, well-trained dog wearing an ugly Christmas sweater made her chuckle.

Mary Grace thought of all the times she'd tracked down Chief of Staff Hensley and stuck a microphone in his face. She was known on the Hill as a shark when she was after a story. She had always thought highly of him and just couldn't imagine him doing something as heinous as selling state secrets to the enemy. But then again, she had exposed other politicians for things that surprised her after uncovering the truth. Most politicians were good actors, but Hensley had a sterling record. No blemishes that she could find in the past when dealing with him on various other issues.

She glanced over her shoulder toward the cockpit—the door was still closed—then back at the laptop. Her reporter's gut was telling her that Hensley may be a pawn, much like Bobby, but if she did what she was thinking about doing, Ned would probably strangle her.

Her gut had never steered her wrong, so she started typing an email. She'd send it to Hensley, giving just enough information to motivate him into meeting with her privately. That way she could study his reactions in person. She vaguely mentioned that she had come across information that could destroy his career, and if he wanted to talk, he could contact her at home later this evening. She sent the email and sat back, wondering just how bad Ned's wrath would be. Well, no time like the present to find out.

She stood, opened the door to the cockpit, took a seat

in the copilot's chair and stared out the front window. His low voice startled her when he spoke.

"You've been up to something."

She immediately took offense, even though she *had* been up to something. "You have absolutely no reason to say something like that."

He stared at her until she squirmed in her seat.

"Let's just say I got the ball rolling before we land in DC. We never really came up with a plan and I know this town and the people on the Hill better than you do. I work here."

She couldn't hear his teeth grinding, but he looked ready to break a tooth, his jaw was so tight.

"Let's hear it," he ground out.

She shot him an exasperated look. "It's not as if you have a better plan. As far as I remember, we really hadn't made any plans at all except to head to DC and stomp in the middle of the hornets' nest and see how many wasps come flying out."

His jaw relaxed and his lips curled at the corners. He seldom smiled and her heart opened just a little wider every time it happened. It made her happy to see him happy, and wasn't that just about as sappy as a girl could get?

"Stomp on a hornets' nest?"

She shrugged. "It's a Southern saying. Anyway, I decided to poke the bear, so to speak." She stopped talking when he gave her a sideways glance. She cleared her throat. "Sorry, I'll try to stop using euphemisms. Anyway, I got to thinking about Hensley. I've interviewed him on the Hill and decided to send him an email, insinuating I've come across something that might have a negative impact on his career."

She waited for his reaction and he didn't disappoint.

"You what?" he exploded. "Mary Grace, whoever is behind this are killers. They want to eliminate any loose ends and that includes you."

Trying to lighten the tension, she tilted her head. "Why, Ned, I didn't know you cared."

His jaw started working again and she almost wished his face were still covered in bushy hair. Her mountain man. She shook her head. No, not *her* mountain man. He would never be her mountain man. With that sobering thought, she apologized.

"Okay, I'm sorry I jumped the gun without discussing it with you first. We're in this together and I didn't act like a team player."

His shoulders finally relaxed, but when he glanced at her, she saw something that resembled guilt in his eyes, but he quickly recovered. She was an excellent observer and didn't try to talk herself out of what she knew she had seen.

"Uh-huh. You're giving me grief, but you've also done something. I take my apology back."

His lips bloomed into a full smile, but Mary Grace knew she'd probably never see that smile again if her PI came back with proof against Finn.

"You can't take back an apology."

Humor laced his words and her heart fluttered, but she ruthlessly buried the feeling.

"Can, too."

He actually laughed. "You sound like a three-year-old."

She laughed back and added, "Do not."

They both sat there for a minute and the camarade-rie faded away.

"I recruited my brother to help before we touch down in Washington."

Now that piece of information got Mary Grace's attention. "And your brother's name?"

"Not important. What is important is that he has a lot of contacts and he tapped into the rumor mill. He spread the word that I'm dating a journalist who is very interested in what happened to me and Finn."

She gave him an incredulous look. "And you think I shouldn't have contacted Hensley? Your brother just painted a bull's-eye on both our backs."

But then her journalist's brain started churning out possibilities. "Actually, this might work into my plans. If your brother's information hits Washington pretty quick, maybe Hensley will get wind of the rumors and be more willing to meet with me."

"With us."

"Huh?" she said, jerked out of her musings.

"If he wants to meet, it'll have to be with both of us. You don't leave my side."

She almost smiled at his rough command, but before she had a chance to say anything, Ned told her to buckle up, and not long after that the plane's wheels ground against the asphalt. They were in Washington, Mary Grace's home turf.

FIFTEEN

They deboarded the plane and Ned strode toward a parked car waiting for them on the tarmac. Mary Grace started asking questions the minute he put the vehicle in Drive. Her job suited her well. He didn't doubt that everyone she interviewed eventually just gave her the answers she wanted to stop her from badgering them. But on the other hand, he was getting used to her constant chatter. The peaceful solitude he'd enjoyed on his mountain didn't seem quite so enticing any longer.

"Is this a private airport? I assume it's private and that's why you didn't have to go inside and do any paperwork. And who handles leaving the cars that have been waiting for us at the airports?"

She didn't wait for him to answer, but kept talking.

"I'd like to swing by my place first." She gave him the address.

He drove the car into a business parking lot, put the address into his phone, then pulled back onto the street. "We'll have to be careful. The people after us may have your place staked out."

"I thought about that, but it's worth the risk because

Bobby may have been able to slip into my house and leave us some kind of information. Maybe Hensley will have responded to my email by the time we get there, and we can set up a meeting."

"I doubt Bobby would hang around Washington while he's hiding. He's probably all the way across the country by now."

She shrugged. "It's worth a shot and Bobby has a key."

Her eyes lit with determination and something else, something he saw reflected in his own mirror at times: the thrill and excitement of the hunt. His heart flipped and it brought a mix of emotions. The longer he was around Mary Grace, the more he didn't want her to get hurt, but all he could do was his best to protect her. He had to remind himself that as a journalist, she was likely exposed to danger. Maybe not the kind they were facing, but certainly disgruntled and angry people whose crimes she had exposed.

He turned right onto her street and scouted the area. No odd-looking vans or cars parked on the street. Then he noticed the place had an urban feel. It sat just outside DC, the type of place large cities were revitalizing, catering to young professionals. She pointed at two parking places, one of which had a used upscale car parked in it.

"That's my car. I took a cab to the airport when I flew to Jackson Hole, so I wouldn't have to deal with airport parking. Park next to mine. I'm allotted two spaces."

Ned pulled into the spot and cut the engine, searching the area for anything that looked out of place. They appeared to be in the clear. Maybe the people after them never dreamed they'd come to her place. It wasn't logical that they would return. Sitting in Mary Grace's lap, Tinker Bell whined. Mary Grace reached to open her car door, but Ned laid a hand on her arm.

"Wait."

She froze and jerked her head around. "What is it?"

Ned scanned the area one more time. The patio homes were built close together with a small strip of grass in between. There were twelve houses lining the street. He peered over his shoulder at the small playground across the road. He still didn't see anything out of the ordinary, but for some reason his gut told him something was off. It wasn't screaming a warning, but something was going on. It could be that they were just being watched from a distance.

Tinker Bell whined again and Mary Grace spoke with urgency. "She has to be let out and a double whine means it's serious."

"Okay, I'll come around to your door and you stay close while your dog does her business. Then we'll go inside."

Constantly scanning the area, Ned got out of the car and rounded the hood. He huddled her forward in front of him. As soon as they hit the grass, she put TB down and he almost heard the dog heave a sigh of relief. Krieger followed suit and relieved himself, as well.

Ned chuckled when he realized what he was doing. If his old comrades could only see him now. Traveling with a journalist and her rat dog was a unique experience, but one he was enjoying more with every passing moment.

He shielded Mary Grace as they moved toward the tiny front entrance and waited while she unlocked the door. He pulled her close to his side and stopped in the foyer after they entered. He closed and locked the door after his dog followed them in.

"Krieger, check it out."

It was one level and Krieger was back in minutes. He sat in front of Ned—the all-clear signal—and Ned released Mary Grace.

Knowing they were safe for the moment, he became curious about her personal living space. In the past, he found that you could gather a lot of information by studying a person's environment.

In the foyer stood a corner coat tree with a bench seat. He moved forward and prowled through the living/ kitchen area. There were three bedrooms, two small and one master. The master had a private bath and one of the smaller bedrooms had been converted into an office. He estimated about fifteen hundred square feet. Everything smelled and looked new.

He grimaced at the huge Christmas tree and all the decorations peppered throughout the place, but became very interested in the framed pictures lining the mantel on the fake fireplace. After being at her grandmother's house, he'd have thought Mary Grace would be the type of woman who'd want a real messy fireplace.

She came and stood beside him. "I wanted a real fireplace, but they aren't allowed here."

Ned picked up a picture of a teenage girl wearing braces and standing on a bicycle. Beside her, a young boy was straddling a banana seat bike. They both wore wide grins.

She took the picture from his hand and stared at it. "This was right after my mother married Bobby's dad. I was so happy to have a sibling. I was thirteen and had been an only child for all those years, spending most of my time at Gram's."

Ned's heart hammered against his chest as he heard the sadness in her voice. He couldn't help himself, he placed a finger under her chin and lifted her head. Slowly, ever so slowly, telling himself he was all kinds of a fool—but not able to stop—he lowered his lips to hers and the warmth of the kiss began melting the frozen, cynical wall he'd built to protect himself.

He pulled away and gazed into her soft golden eyes, wanting to believe in her with every fiber of his being, but he reminded himself of the item she had found in the shack that she hadn't shared. He retreated instantly. As he stepped back, he didn't miss the hurt in her eyes, but she recovered quickly and took several steps away and cleared her throat.

"Yes, well, I'll look around and see if Bobby left any clues and check my email for a response from Hensley."

She disappeared into her small office. Ned took one step forward, but stopped himself. He shook off the kiss and tender feelings she evoked. Until she came clean, he couldn't trust her and he had to keep his mind clear. He had a job to do.

Hands trembling, Mary Grace slipped into the chair behind her desk and started booting up her computer. Leaning sideways, she peeked into the living area. Ned had his back turned to her and was once again studying the pictures on her mantel.

She stared blankly at the computer screen while it was booting up and thought about that kiss. It had been so warm and precious until he pulled away, mistrust flickering in his eyes. She slumped in her chair. He had every right not to trust her because she was withholding information, even if it was for his own good. Maybe she should just tell him about Bobby's letter, but even if she did, it would probably make matters worse. Mistrust was better than accusations in her opinion.

She typed in her password, went straight to her email account and there sat an email from the private investigator she had hired. She stared at it for a moment, then closed her eyes and prayed not only that God would show her the truth, but that both she and Ned could handle the fallout in a worst-case scenario.

Taking a deep breath, she opened her eyes and clicked the email. She read it twice before closing her eyes once again. It was definitely a worst-case scenario and she had to tell Ned. Now, before things went any further. She briefly wondered why Bobby hadn't been able to find the information himself, but maybe the place where he was hiding didn't have internet service. She swallowed hard and quickly pushed aside the thought that maybe he wasn't alive and able to do the search himself.

Feeling like an old woman, she pushed herself out of her chair and walked into the living room. Ned turned at her approach and lifted a bushy questioning brow. She motioned toward the sofa.

"Let's have a seat."

He moved toward her and stopped so close she could

feel his breath on her face. Gently placing both hands on her arms, he demanded softly, "Tell me."

Mary Grace gazed into those intelligent green eyes of his and wondered if this would be the last time they would be together. Would he leave after she told him what she'd discovered?

"I—I found something at the shack that I haven't shared."

To her surprise, Ned's lips curled at the corners and his expression softened. He led her to the sofa and pulled her down by his side. She felt the warmth emanating from his body, but she shivered in spite of it.

"I've been waiting for you to tell me the truth. I knew you found something at the shack, but I wanted you to tell me on your own, because you trusted me."

"You knew?" she whispered. "Ned, Bobby left me another letter for my eyes only in a place where no one would look. A secret hiding place we used when we were kids. It was behind a loose board in the wall of the shack."

She swallowed again, forcing the words past her lips. "I didn't tell you because I wanted to check out what he had to say before I shared. And after I read it, I didn't want you to get hurt."

His eyes narrowed, but she forced the words out. "Bobby named a second person that he highly suspects is connected to what happened to you and Finn."

Ned was a smart man, and she could almost see his brain churning out the possibilities.

"Go on." His words weren't quite as soft now and his eyes had narrowed.

With tears in her eyes, she lifted her chin and told

him straight, with no embellishments. "Bobby suspects Finn of being involved in selling the state secrets you two were trying to uncover." Before he could explode, she talked fast. "On the plane, I emailed a private investigator I've used in the past. I trust him implicitly. He ran a deep search on Finn. Half a million dollars was placed in an offshore account in Finn's name two days before the failed mission. Another half a million was deposited into the same account two days after the mission."

Her heart in her throat, Mary Grace found that she couldn't breathe while she watched a drastic change come over Ned. He didn't make a sound, seemingly frozen into place until his intense green gaze landed directly on her.

"And you expect me to believe something your brother wrote in a letter to his sister? A brother probably trying to save his own skin? You expect me to believe that Finn, a man I grew up with and have known all my life, betrayed me? You think he planned an event that would place him in a wheelchair for the rest of his life?"

Mary Grace shivered. Ned didn't sound like the gruff, exasperated mountain man she'd come to know. The affable Scottish guy was long gone, too. She didn't recognize the man sitting beside her, staring at her with accusing eyes. He had kept this part of himself hidden from her: the intelligent warrior willing to die for what he believed in, and he didn't believe in Mary Grace and Bobby. He believed in Finn.

Mary Grace hardened her resolve, fell back on her professionalism and stared him in the eye. "I have proof. My PI found the deposits made in Finn's name."

Ned's lips curled into a cynical smile. "Let's see. What is it you made me promise about Bobby? That someone could have set him up and I should wait to make sure before I go after him? Don't you think the same thing could have been done to Finn?"

Mary Grace had to concede the point, but her reporter's gut was screaming that Finn had betrayed Ned.

She gave a stiff nod. "Fine, I agree. It's possible that Finn could have been set up. We'll have to follow all the leads and see what shakes out."

She softened her voice. "Listen, Ned, I know it's hard to believe that Finn could do something like this—"

His words sliced into the air, effectively cutting her off. "Finn did not do this and I'll prove it."

Mary Grace peered into his beautiful eyes, eyes that had previously warmed her heart, but the only thing reflected back at her now was a green as hard and brittle as colored glass. He was lost to her, if they even had a chance to begin with. Even if they found Finn innocent, she doubted Ned would ever forgive her for putting him through this. But she knew, deep down, that for some unknown reason Finn had betrayed his best friend, and it was something Ned might never recover from. Ned had trust issues and this would place him out of her reach forever. He'd crawl back to his mountain and hibernate for years.

Gram had always taught her to keep moving forward, no matter what was going on in her life, and Mary Grace did just that. She'd had plenty of practice with her mother and stepfather. When she was a teenager, she sometimes wanted to crawl into a hole and stay there, but Gram always pulled out her Bible and reminded Mary Grace that God loved her, and stood beside her, no matter what.

She wrapped her mind around those old scriptures—they gave her strength—and straightened her shoulders.

"Do we stay together, or would you prefer we handle our investigations separately?"

He smiled, and it wasn't a team-player smile. Mary Grace almost laughed at the thought. Ned definitely wasn't a team player. She briefly wondered how he would fare at one of those team-building conferences that companies made their employees attend. He'd probably scare the daylights out of everyone there.

She stopped her semi-hysterical train of thought, knowing from the past it was a coping mechanism unique to her.

"Oh, we'll stay together. You aren't leaving my sight until we find your brother."

And wasn't that just nice? But she had to remind herself this was hard on Ned, too.

"Fine, but, Ned? I really do hope both Bobby and Finn are completely innocent in all of this. I'm sorry I had to tell you what I found out about Finn, but it had to be done."

Calling herself all kinds of silly, Mary Grace felt the waves of pain coming off him and she found herself still wanting to soothe the heartache he was experiencing due to the information she had unearthed.

But Gram had taught her to be practical, and no matter her feelings for Ned, she had to find Bobby, make sure he was alright, and then she would expose the person, or persons, responsible for what had happened to Ned and Finn, and if Finn was involved, well, God would have to take care of the rest.

SIXTEEN

Ned refused to believe that Finn was in league with traitors to the country and had betrayed him. Finn hadn't had the best family life growing up, but they had saved each another's lives on more than one occasion when they were in the army. Someone had to have set Finn up. The alternative was unthinkable.

He counted himself fortunate that he hadn't completely fallen for the woman sitting next to him. Or had he? No, he wouldn't even allow that possibility to enter his mind. He had to remember her main goal was to prove her brother innocent, and if she could point the finger elsewhere, it was to her benefit.

It felt like a giant fist was squeezing the blood from his heart, but he focused his mind on the mission ahead and compartmentalized all other emotions.

He ruthlessly ignored the sadness on Mary Grace's face. "Did you receive an email from Hensley?" He almost winced as he heard his own voice, so similar to his brother's clipped, terse tone.

She searched his face one more time before shrugging her shoulders, and that bothered him, that she could dismiss him so easily. "No, I haven't heard from him, but he may be tied up with official business. I say we grab some lunch. I'll send another email asking him to meet us somewhere away from prying eyes. There's a small park just outside the city that's fairly secluded."

He nodded his assent and watched as she shuffled toward her small office. He stayed seated and gazed at the pictures on the mantel once more. Just how far would Mary Grace go to save her brother? Restless, he rose and began pacing through the dainty town house. He could search online, see if he could track Bobby himself, but Mary Grace's brother was a computer wizard and knew enough to stay offline if he didn't want to be found. He could also run a deep check into Finn, but that would mean admitting he didn't trust his friend.

He stopped in the foyer and lifted his chin. A few seconds later, Krieger was by his side and the dog released a low growl. It was an alert, not a full-blown warning. Ned opened the front door and scanned the area. A few kids were on swings in the playground under the watchful eyes of their mothers. He remembered the odd feeling he had gotten when they arrived. It hadn't been a feeling of immediate danger, just that something was off.

He spied a man walking his dog down the street, but that was it. He closed the door. Maybe Krieger was reacting to Ned's own turbulent emotions. Dogs were very sensitive to their handlers. Mary Grace came up behind him. She was dressed to leave.

"I heard back from Hensley. He'll meet us at the park at six o'clock. I'd like to see his reaction in person. We'll pick up something to eat while we wait."

She acted like she wanted to add something, but her lips tightened. Ned found himself aching to smooth the worry lines from her forehead, but he only nodded and grabbed his coat from the rack in the corner.

TB was already tucked safely into the dog carrier and Krieger trotted out behind them. Mary Grace swirled around to face him. She had her car keys in her hand.

"After everything that's happened, maybe it would be best if we part company. If you'll give me your cell number, I'll keep you apprised of any information I uncover and I'd appreciate it if you would return the favor."

Caught off guard by the sudden change of plans, he stood there and just stared at her, his mind a whirlwind of emotions. The woman had turned his life inside out. He was torn between wanting to distance himself from her and aching to glue himself to her side forever.

Receiving no response, she gazed at him one last time, then pivoted on her heel toward her car. Frozen to the spot, he watched as she opened the car door and slipped inside. Away from him, that's all he could think about. Through the side window, he watched her pull TB from the carrier and place the dog on the passenger seat. She leaned forward to insert the key into the ignition and warning bells exploded in Ned's head. Mary Grace's car had been sitting there the whole time she'd been gone. Plenty of opportunity for someone to tamper with it. The feeling that something was off crystallized in his mind.

Both he and Krieger were already moving when she turned the key and the engine caught. Rounding the hood of the car, he ripped her door open, pulled her out of the car and made a flying leap into the air. He heard Krieger behind him and dearly hoped his dog would save the rat. Mary Grace would never get over losing her dog.

He might not trust her, and he was very angry with her, but he didn't want her to die.

About fifteen seconds after they hit the ground and cleared the car—Mary Grace protected beneath him—a small explosion blew through the air and light debris stung his back as it seared through his shirt and jacket.

Before he could catch his breath and assess the situation, a sharp elbow almost caved in his trachea as Mary Grace fought her way out from under him. Shifting his weight off her, she scrambled to her feet and frantically swiveled her head around.

"Tinker Bell! Where's my dog?" she shouted.

Ned got to his feet and breathed a sigh of relief when Krieger padded toward them with TB dangling from his mouth, hanging inside the ugly Christmas sweater. At least it was good for something.

Ned scanned the area for any lingering danger while Mary Grace gingerly removed her dog from Krieger's jaws and gently soothed TB's nerves. After making sure her dog was okay, she dropped to her knees and threw her arms around Krieger. She praised Ned's dog and told him he was a hero. It was the first time Ned had ever been jealous of his dog.

Disgusted with himself, he turned away from the tender scene and scanned the area once more, but didn't sense anyone lurking about. He was glad to see no one on the playground. They must have left while he and Mary Grace were inside the town house. He wasn't surprised to hear sirens in the distance. An explosion, even a small one, wasn't something this neighborhood would be familiar with and a neighbor had probably called the cops.

Mary Grace got to her feet and walked slowly toward him, resolution written on her face. She stopped in front of him, her precious dog still trembling in her arms.

"You saved my life and Krieger saved Tinker Bell. I thank you for that." She took a deep breath and lifted a defiant chin. "I know it was wrong of me to withhold information from you, but I honestly did it so you wouldn't get hurt. If the PI I hired hadn't found anything on Finn, I never would have mentioned Bobby's letter to you." She took what appeared to be a defensive step back. But before she could say anything else, a city police cruiser pulled to the curb in front of her driveway.

Mary Grace watched the policeman walk briskly toward them, keeping a sharp, questioning eye on Krieger. Ned mumbled low so only she could hear before the cop got within hearing distance.

"Don't say anything, let me handle this."

She nodded her assent. The day was waning, and they had an important meeting to make in a few hours. If Ned and his connections could move this along, it was more than fine with her.

Ned moved toward the cop and held out a small piece of paper. Naturally curious, Mary Grace moved close enough to hear.

"If you'll call this number, everything will be taken care of."

Suspicion filled the cop's eyes until he glanced down

at the paper. He stepped away, never turning his back to them and pulled out a phone. He spoke to someone for a few minutes, then ended the call and moved back toward them. He scrutinized Ned for a moment, nodded, handed the piece of paper back, got in his car and left.

Mary Grace was incredulous. She stared at Ned. "What just happened?"

He grinned at her, and just like that, they were back on even ground. He stared at her for a moment, as if he wanted to say something, then shook his head.

"I gave him the direct line to the CIA and a guy I know there who handles situations such as this. Let's get going." He went quiet for a moment. "This looks like a professional job. Just enough of a boom to get the job done, but not enough to attract major attention."

She followed Ned to the car that had been left at the airport for them and they loaded up. She rubbed the top of Tinker Bell's head and the white silky fur soothed Mary Grace. Dogs really were good therapy. Krieger jumped in after Ned opened the rear door and hung his head over the back of Mary Grace's seat.

She grinned, then sighed at the expression of adoration in the big dog's eyes as he stared at Tinker Bell. The animals reminded Mary Grace of her and Ned in reverse. She hoped she didn't wear that sappy expression when she gazed at Ned.

Ned folded his large body into the driver's seat and started the car. Putting forth great effort, she told him of a good local restaurant where they could pick up something fairly fast. Everything was somewhat back to normal. She stared out the window, thankful to be alive.

* * *

They'd eaten and arrived at the park an hour early. As Ned scoped out the area, Mary Grace waited in the car. She'd promised to keep all the doors locked and be ready to start the car and leave if anything suspicious happened.

Sitting behind the wheel, she glanced at Krieger in the rearview mirror. "Like I'd leave him at the first sign of trouble."

Krieger rumbled back, obviously unhappy at being left behind to protect Mary Grace and Tinker Bell. Fifteen minutes later, Ned cleared the woods and Mary Grace scooted across the console so he could have the driver's seat. A whoosh of cold air flowed into the car with him.

"Everything's clear. The temperature's dropping."

"Well, it is December." She sighed longingly. "Christmas is almost here. I hope we resolve this soon. I'd like to spend Christmas with Gram—" she hesitated to finish her sentence, almost afraid to upset their unspoken, tacit agreement to work together "—and Bobby."

Broodingly, he stared out the windshield as a flake of snow drifted onto the glass. "One step at a time," was all he said.

Tentatively, trying to make conversation, but also very curious about this secretive man, she asked, "Do you usually spend Christmas with your family in Jackson Hole?"

Surprisingly, he answered, "The house in Jackson Hole is our home base in America. My family travels a lot, but we try to get everyone together in the same country for Christmas."

That didn't tell her much of anything, but it didn't surprise her. She briefly wondered if he would ever trust her enough to tell her about his family.

She couldn't help herself; she had to throw in another more personal question. "And do you still believe in the true reason for the season?"

His large hands gripped the steering wheel. "God allowed someone to betray me and Finn, and He allowed Finn to get injured." He paused and relaxed his fingers. "I come from a family of believers, but during my time in the army, I witnessed so-called religious figures in many countries commit atrocious crimes, all in the name of their religion."

Mart Grace nodded sagely. "Just what I thought."

He snapped his head around. "What?"

She twisted sideways in her seat and smiled at him. "It's okay, Ned, God understands you're angry right now, but He will bring everything to rights. In the end, even if it's not what we envisioned, it will be the right thing, the best thing for us." She paused, gathering her thoughts because this was so important, especially if they ended up proving Finn, his best friend, had betrayed him. "Ned, God will reveal the truth about everything, and we, as believers, have to accept it."

He smiled and it wasn't a nice smile. "So you're going to be able to accept it, just like that, if we prove your brother is partially responsible for what happened to my best friend?"

Mary Grace jerked her head back as if she'd just been slapped. Would she be able to accept it if Bobby ended up in jail? She didn't have time to ponder the question because they both sat up straight when a car pulled into the empty parking lot, the fluttering snow having sent the last of the park visitors home before their guest arrived.

Ned reached for his door handle. "Stay in the car while I make sure it's safe, then you can join us."

Mary Grace protested him going alone.

Exasperation written on his face, Ned said, "Would you, just for once, do what I say? I'm trying to protect you."

She leaned back in her seat with a huff. "Fine, but don't ask him anything until I get there. I want to gauge his reaction."

Finally, she noted a spark of humor in his eyes. "Don't worry. I know you're the expert talker. I'll give you full control after I make sure it's safe."

Mary Grace nodded her assent and he climbed from the car. They had parked in a corner of the lot under some bare tree limbs, but Hensley spotted Ned coming toward him as soon as he got out of his car. Not willing to take a chance on Ned's life, Mary Grace reached over the console and quietly opened the driver's door.

"Krieger, protect Ned."

If a dog could smile, Krieger was grinning as he flew over the seat and jumped out of the car. Mary Grace was impressed when the dog took to the woods and quietly circled around behind Chief of Staff Hensley.

She watched the man approach Ned and thought the meeting was going nicely—until Hensley pulled a handgun from inside his coat and pointed it straight at Ned's heart.

SEVENTEEN

Ned wasn't surprised when Hensley pulled a gun on him. Under the circumstances, he would have done the same thing in the other man's shoes and would have respected Hensley less if he hadn't taken the precaution, but that didn't mean he trusted the man. Not at all.

He raised his hands in the air, just enough to show the man he meant no harm, but he'd palmed a knife inside one fist in case things went downhill fast. One throw to the trachea and Hensley would be dead.

The president's chief of staff kept his eyes on Ned. The man was definitely out of his element.

But Ned never underestimated anyone.

Hensley spoke first. "Do I know you?"

He was studying Ned intently. But before he could respond, Ned was startled to see Krieger lope out of the woods and sneak up behind Hensley. His dog assumed attack position and stared at Ned, awaiting a command.

Ned wanted to close his eyes in frustration, knowing this was Mary Grace's doing, and he was proven right when she hopped out of their car and came striding across the parking lot. His heart in his throat, he wanted to strangle her and throw his body in front of her at the same time. The woman continuously elicited conflicting emotions in him, even now when he needed to defuse the tense situation in front of him.

From inside the dog carrier, TB gave a bark of greeting as Mary Grace hurried to his side. He was angry, but also impressed with the way she quickly defused the situation.

She kind of puffed her hand at Hensley. "Sir, please put the gun away. There's no need for that and you're scaring Tinker Bell to death."

With disbelieving eyes, both men stared at the happy fluffy white rat dog with its tiny head sticking out the top of the dog carrier snuggled against Mary Grace's chest.

She made a show of calming the already perfectly calm dog and Ned almost barked out a laugh. Even though he still wanted to strangle her, he admired her pizzazz.

She stared pointedly at Hensley until the chief of staff finally lowered his weapon to his side, but he didn't put the gun away. She gifted him with her big Georgian smile.

"Now, I've interviewed you in the past, and you know I'm a trusted journalist. I just need a few moments of your time."

Now that the high probability of danger was past, Hensley gave both of them a nervous look, then ran slim fingers through his thinning hair and cleared his throat.

"I want to know what this is all about."

Mary Grace held out both hands. "I really just have one important question." Ned marveled at the change that came over Mary Grace. Her jaw hardened and her eyes narrowed.

"Are you trying to kill me or my brother?"

Hensley's brows arched toward his hairline and he clumsily placed his gun back inside his jacket.

"What? Why on earth would I want to kill a White House press correspondent? I don't even know your brother. And what does this have to do with your email? You said you had information that might negatively impact my career. That's the only reason I came here."

Hensley took a deep breath, like he was settling in for a long-winded tirade, but Mary Grace cut him off at the knees. Still alert, Ned relaxed a tad and enjoyed watching Mary Grace do what she did best: talk. She placed her hand on TB's head and went for the soft touch.

"Chief of Staff Hensley, it really is for your benefit that I contacted you. You see, Ned is here to protect me, and someone has made several attempts on my life. During the course of my investigation, I came across information that led me to you. You have been targeted in a cover-up that goes to the top of the pecking order in Washington. If the information becomes public, you will be ruined whether you're involved or not. You know how it works."

She shook her head sadly and Ned bit back another grin.

"I have interviewed you, and my resources tell me you work hard and have never been involved in any kind of cover-up."

Indignant, Hensley lifted his chin. "I don't know where you received your information, but I'll do everything in my power to help you find the culprits. My background is clean, and I plan to keep it that way."

Hensley stared at Ned, an assessing look in his eyes. Ned knew the moment the man snapped the puzzle pieces together. The pieces connecting Mary Grace and a cover-up to a man named Ned. Hensley was high enough on the power grid in Washington to be aware of Ned's reputation. His eyes widened slightly, the only indication he gave at figuring out who Ned was, a man known only as Ned by a small, select few. A man who worked for the CIA, but whose identity was kept quiet. Ned didn't mind being partially revealed because he never intended to do undercover work again. He was leaving the CIA for good. After what had happened with Finn, and the betrayal they both experienced, he'd never trust anyone enough to put his or anyone else's life on the line again.

Ned didn't know if Mary Grace saw the indicator, but as sharp as she was, he'd have been surprised if she missed anything. He had his answer a second later.

With a winsome smile, she indicated with her hand. "I see you understand what's at stake. After speaking with you, my gut tells me you're a pawn in this nefarious conspiracy, maybe set up to take the fall for something you didn't do, but if you work with me, I hope to expose the person, or persons, responsible. We've had someone spread rumors and specific information in Washington. Information we hope will bring those responsible to the surface. There's the possibility you might receive a small amount of bad publicity, but I'll make sure you end up a hero in the press."

Hensley's face literally turned red with anger. "I don't

know what's going on, and I wouldn't give credence to anything you're saying if it weren't for the man standing beside you, but I'll play along for the time being because I don't want my reputation torn to shreds."

Mary Grace smiled, but the tone of her words ensured he understood she meant business. "I said I'll make sure everything works out right for you."

Hensley's face went from red to white. " I'll do my part to help with anything you need. I'm a man of the people."

Mary Grace said briskly, "Good."

Ned was very impressed, and he realized if her brother were anything like his sister, it was no wonder the CIA had recruited him. Mary Grace was the epitome of intrigue.

Behind the men, Krieger stood at attention and pointed his nose toward a bare tree line. Ned didn't see anything, but he trusted his dog's instincts. "Krieger, check the perimeter."

Their visitor was visibly shaken when he realized a huge German shepherd had been sitting behind him the entire time.

"I want everyone to casually walk to their cars and leave quickly. My dog gave me an imminent danger signal."

They dispersed swiftly. Ned kept his eyes trained on the wooded area Krieger had pointed out while herding Mary Grace to the car. As he scanned the tree line, the setting sun glinted off the long barrel of a gun. He looked closer and saw an unusual lump about midway up the tree. A sharpshooter. Ned moved fast, just as the first bullet barely missed them and pinged off the car.

"Mary Grace, get in the car. Now!" he shouted as he whipped his pistol out and started running across the parking lot while firing toward the guy hidden in the tree. Hensley turned, saw what was happening and pulled out his gun. Ned prayed Hensley was innocent in all of this, because if the shooter was someone he'd brought with him, Ned and Mary Grace were in deep trouble.

Mary Grace dove into the driver's seat. Her hands shook as she turned the key in the ignition. It would be her fault if Ned got shot. She berated herself for always being so stubborn. She had set up this meeting and if someone got killed, she would carry the weight of that for the rest of her life.

The car roared to life and she hit the gas pedal right when Hensley lifted his gun. She'd have no qualms about running the man down if he dared to turn his weapon on Ned, but when she got closer to them, she realized Hensley was trying to help. Both men were shooting toward the trees.

She whooshed out a breath of relief as she slammed on the brakes, skidding to a halt right behind Ned. His gun still in his hand, and his eyes scouring the area, he opened the driver's car door.

"Scoot over."

She wanted to argue that she was perfectly capable of driving the car, but decided this wasn't the time to argue. She slid into the passenger seat and yelped when Krieger leaped through the open door and landed in the back seat. She breathed a sigh of relief when she saw Hensley running toward his car, then climbing in to safety.

Gun still in hand, Ned slid into the car, put it in Drive and drove with one hand, his eyes never leaving the surrounding area. He didn't slip the weapon into his jacket until they were well clear of the park.

Both cars had escaped without anyone getting hurt and Mary Grace closed her eyes.

"Thank You, dear Lord, for protecting us." She breathed the prayer out loud.

She lifted her lids and stared out the front window. That had been a close call. Too close. She laid a hand on Tinker Bell's head, as much to soothe herself as her dog and released a nervous chuckle.

"Well, I'd say Hensley is in the clear. Bobby's information must have been wrong."

Without saying a word, Ned lifted his brows and glanced at her before looking at the road again. She blew out a breath of frustration.

"I know what you're thinking."

He didn't say a word. He was going to make this hard on her, but she really didn't blame him.

"Fine, maybe Bobby was wrong about Finn, too, but we still need to follow up on that money in the offshore account in Finn's name."

The man-of-few-words only nodded, and it was maddening.

"Aren't you going to say something? Anything?"

He stayed quiet.

"Fine, I was wrong to put the two of us and Hensley at risk like that and I want to apologize. It's just that I'm so worried about Bobby and I really want to find whoever is after us. I have to follow every lead, but I could have handled this differently. Safer."

She stared out the window, expecting his condemnation, but was shocked when she sneaked a peek in his direction, unable to believe her eyes.

Mountain Man was grinning.

He shocked her when he finally spoke. "The meeting was the right thing to do."

Her first reaction was relief that Ned didn't think she'd messed up big time by placing them in danger, but then she slumped in her seat, thinking about what she planned to do. Her gut declared that Finn was involved, but it was also screaming another name, and if Mary Grace was right, things were about to get much more dangerous than she'd ever dreamed.

This time she refused to accuse anyone Ned trusted without proof. She prayed he wouldn't be angry when he learned what she was really preparing to set in motion, but what did it matter? It was very unlikely they'd ever have any kind of a relationship, anyway. There were too many things standing between them.

It was also the story of a lifetime. She glanced at Ned and wondered where they'd be after this was all over. Would he learn to trust her, or would he walk away forever when he found out she'd once again withheld information?

EIGHTEEN

Ned gripped the steering wheel harder as snowflakes swirled and darkness descended, relieved only by the streetlights as they crossed the bridge over the Potomac River.

"Where are we going? I know it's not safe to go to my town house."

He glanced in the rearview mirror, but didn't see anyone following them. "I have a small town house in Washington I keep available for whenever I'm in town. Excluding family, no one knows about it, so we can regroup there."

Curiosity laced her next question. "Do you spend much time in Washington?"

After the close call at the park, Mary Grace didn't seem upset. The woman was pretty remarkable, but Ned ignored the tiny spark in his heart robustly trying to grow into a flame and broached a subject Mary Grace wouldn't be happy to hear instead of answering.

"I have a proposition."

She slid him a sideways glance. "I don't like the sound of this."

He plowed forward, even though he knew it was probably futile. "The further we get into this thing, the more dangerous it becomes, and I think you should stay behind, where it's safe."

She twisted sideways in her seat and exploded right on cue, the gold in her eyes sparking fire. "Oh, no, you don't. You might live like a Neanderthal on that mountain of yours, and you might think like one, but I've been taking care of myself for a long time and I refuse to hide in safety while you take all the risks. Taking risks is part of my job description and you need me to put my plan into action."

Mary Grace reminded him of a frontier woman, soft on the outside but tough at the core, able to endure just about anything thrown her way.

He grinned, knowing it would drive her crazy. "It was worth a try."

He wasn't surprised when she socked him in the arm and followed that with a fierce glare.

"Just what exactly is your plan? You were pretty vague with Hensley."

She plopped back in her seat and became quiet. Ned sensed her plotting. He was becoming so attuned to her, it was unsettling.

"I want to do some interviews that will hopefully prompt those responsible for this mess to make a move. We'll refine it when we get to the town house."

For some reason, Ned couldn't shake the feeling that she wasn't telling him everything, but he ignored it because he wanted to trust her as he hadn't trusted anyone in a long time.

He pulled into a middle-class neighborhood and

pressed the automatic garage door opener he kept on his personal key chain as he guided the car into the driveway of a benign town house, built identical to the others surrounding it. That's why he'd bought the place. Nothing about it stood out and the neighbors kept to themselves.

The garage door closed behind them and automatic lights flicked on.

Mary Grace shifted in her seat. "Somehow, I just can't imagine Mountain Man living in a town house."

Her humor had his lips twitching and his mind shifted gears. He didn't want to think about someone trying to kill them, or about Finn being in a wheelchair for the rest of his life, or the gut feeling that she was plotting again. He'd hidden it, but the shooting at the park had shaken him to the core. He was comfortable with danger, but the thought of anything happening to Mary Grace, the possibility of a world without her in it, even if they weren't together, was unthinkable.

Even though he knew it was a mistake, because after this was over they'd go their separate ways, and he wasn't ready to admit that his feelings might be something... more for Mary Grace, he wanted to kiss her—right here, right now, as affirmation of their survival after the shooting. When she'd driven the car toward Hensley at the park with fierce determination blazing in her eyes, Ned's heart had almost jumped out of his chest. First in fear for her, and then because he realized she was risking her life to protect him.

Her eyes widened when he slowly reached across the seat and pulled TB from the dog carrier pouch. He placed the dog in the back seat with Krieger and twisted back around. Mary Grace didn't move a muscle until he lifted her chin with a finger.

He was very seldom surprised or caught off guard, but he was startled when she jerked forward and wrapped her arms around his neck, pulling his head forward. When she placed her lips against his, Ned felt as if he had come home. The world was no longer filled with evil and betrayal, but…possibilities. His heart beat wildly as her kiss brought hope for the future. A future he never dared dream possible for a man like him, a man who'd seen too much of the depraved side of humanity.

Even in the middle of an impossible dream, Ned's subconscious instincts stayed focused and he immediately sensed another presence. In one swift move, he pulled away from Mary Grace, shoved her head down, whipped his pistol from inside his jacket and pointed it at the man standing beside his car window.

He immediately recognized the person and so did Mary Grace. She grabbed Ned's arm and forced the gun down.

The joy in her voice reflected a far different reaction than Ned's.

"Bobby!"

Mary Grace scrambled out of the car and ran around the hood toward Bobby. She threw her arms around him and squeezed tight. "Thank You, Lord! Thank You for protecting my brother."

She pulled back and studied him intently. He was tall and lanky, and although he was twenty-five years old, he still only managed to grow what resembled peach fuzz on his face. He had unkempt dark blond hair and he pushed his glasses up the bridge of his nose in a familiar, endearing way. Some might call him a nerd, but to Mary Grace he was one of the sweetest, most honest people she knew.

A blush worked its way up his neck and spread over his face when he reached behind him and tugged a woman forward. With a mixture of shock and confusion, Mary Grace said, "Fran?"

During their short reunion, Ned had slipped out of the car and was leaning against the driver's door. He gave his niece a hard stare.

"Yes, Fran, what are you doing with Mary Grace's brother?"

Before Fran had a chance to answer, Bobby stepped forward and squared off in front of Ned, who towered over him, reminding Mary Grace of the large, immovable mountain he lived on. Bobby surprised Mary Grace, first with his bravery, because Ned wasn't the type of person most people would directly challenge, and second by the accusation in her brother's voice.

"You were kissing my sister."

Ned growled back, "What are you doing with my niece?"

Mary Grace had always been the one to protect Bobby, not the other way around. She appreciated his standing up for her, but Ned could squish her brother like a bug if he chose to. Determined to get everyone settled down, she stepped between the men.

"Let's take this inside. I'll make some coffee and we can talk."

Bobby looked like he wanted to punch Ned and Ned looked like he wanted to wring answers out of Bobby's thin neck, which would easily snap under Ned's large hands.

She was grateful when Fran stepped forward and grabbed Bobby's hand. She led him toward a door Mary Grace assumed opened into the town house. Ned's eyes flared hot when he saw Bobby's and Fran's interlocked hands.

Mary Grace knew she had to defuse the volatile situation. They followed Bobby and Fran through the door Fran had opened after punching in a code. Ned must give his family access to his properties.

They entered through the kitchen and Mary Grace was disappointed to find nothing personal in the area. The inside of the town house was just as bland as the outside. The living room sat across a small hallway from the kitchen and it appeared as if two bedrooms and baths made up the rest of the small space.

Bobby and Fran sat on the sofa and Mary Grace winced when she noticed they were still holding hands. Not because she didn't like Fran, but because of Ned's reaction. It was obvious he was protective of his niece and Mary Grace had experienced his fierce protectiveness.

Ned took a seat in a cushy chair, leaned back and crossed his arms over his chest like a big grumpy bear. The two men glared at one another and Fran looked miserable.

"Let me make some coffee and then we'll talk," Mary Grace said.

Mr. Man-of-Few-Words laid down the law. "No coffee. We talk now, and it better be good."

Mary Grace knew when to gracefully give in. She

took the only other chair in the room. Tinker Bell jumped in her lap, Krieger lay on the floor beside her and she started the ball rolling. Better coming from her than Ned.

She managed a wobbly smile. "Bobby, I'm so glad you're alright. I was worried."

Bobby tore his gaze away from Ned. "I didn't mean for any of this to happen. You know I would never intentionally put you in danger."

"Of course you wouldn't," she responded swiftly, knowing in her heart that his words were true. Bobby was naive and too trusting and at times people tended to abuse that sterling quality.

Bobby glanced at Fran, tightened his grip on her hand and sat up straighter. "I know you've had to pull me out of a few scrapes over the years, and I appreciate that, sis, but I'm a man now. I'm responsible for my own actions."

Mary Grace wanted to cheer and cry at the same time. Bobby had grown up and she had to accept that fact. It was no longer her job to look out for bullies and people who might hurt him.

Ned leaned forward in a threatening manner, placing his elbows on his thighs, and Mary Grace forced herself not to jump into the fray again. Bobby was right. He was twenty-five. Time to stand on his own. She suspected Fran had something to do with Bobby's newfound courage and she applauded the woman for bringing her brother out of his timid shell.

"I suggest you start at the beginning, and I advise you to leave nothing out because not only have you placed your sister in danger, somehow you have dragged my niece into this mess."

Ned's words hung in the room like shards of ice, but Mary Grace settled back in her chair. She sent up a quick prayer that this would end well, because judging by the way Fran and Bobby were gazing at each other, she just might be involved in Ned's life whether he wanted her there or not. She felt a momentary pang at the thought, but focused her attention on Bobby's explanation.

He gazed directly at Ned and Mary Grace's heart burst with pride.

"As I'm sure you know, I was recruited straight out of college by the CIA based on certain aptitude tests I took. They offered to pay off my school loans if I agreed to work for them for five years." He smiled at Fran before continuing. "I only have one more year left, and after that I'd like to create Christian video games based on Bible stories."

"I'm not interested in what you do in the future, but what you've done in the past. Your future will be determined by that," Ned interjected in a harsh voice.

Mary Grace gave her brother credit, instead of squirming in his seat, he faced Ned like a man.

"My job is to analyze information and occasionally assist with missions that require help with computerized security cameras and such. They never explain what, or where, the mission is, just what my small part of the job will be and when I should do it."

Ned gave him a hard look and Bobby's words came out faster.

"What no one is aware of is that I have another talent. I love puzzles and I can pretty much decipher any code. Everything I worked on had information they didn't want me to see in code." He shrugged. "I guess they assumed it was safe from prying eyes."

Ned nodded. "Go on."

Bobby took a deep breath and continued, "They put me on standby—which means I had to be at my desk, ready to move—to disable some security cameras in a certain art gallery. I got curious and searched for the file that fit the timeline of my assignment. I found it, and when I realized what I was looking at, I was shocked. Everyone I work with had heard of *Ned* but no one knew his true identity. I'd heard all kinds of stories about the man, but didn't believe half of them. It was impossible for one man to have done all that."

Ned leaned back in his chair in a relaxed position, but Mary Grace knew him well enough to know he was strung as taut as a bowstring. She watched both men, willing Bobby to move it along. Curiosity was eating her alive.

Bobby finally lifted his head and Mary Grace detected a touch of fear in his eyes. "I found out who Ned really is. Who you are."

Mary Grace drew in a sharp breath. Bobby knew everything about Ned!

He went on, "I noticed something else in the file, something odd that caught my eye."

"Aye? And what was that, Bobby?"

"Your escape exit from the location. There wasn't one."

Mary Grace jerked when Ned tore out of his chair and started pacing the floor. "That's because we were supposed to be dead."

Mary Grace swallowed hard and waited for Bobby to continue.

"That was my assessment. I didn't know what to do, or who to trust, so for a long time, I carefully poked around and finally located another file, one that had been approved and showed your escape route. I assume that's the one they sent you. At that point, I knew I didn't have much time before I was discovered looking in places I shouldn't, but I was able to find several emails sent between Hensley and Finn. It was made to appear that the two men were conversing about your current mission, but something didn't feel right. It's easy to send an email from someone else's server if you know what you're doing. I didn't have time to read them all. I stayed offline the whole time I was in hiding so no one could track me, so I never had a chance to dig deeper."

Bobby swallowed hard. "When the mission went down, I disabled all the cameras like I was supposed to, but left one live." He rubbed his right temple, as if reliving the scene, then looked up. "Not that it proved who was responsible, but I did see what happened. You were set up. I didn't record the event because I knew if I was right, my superiors would be able to track the recording on my computer. People who work for the CIA have been known to disappear.

"I don't know if Hensley and your friend, Finn, were set up to take the fall, or if they were actually involved. I got out of there as fast as I could. It was too dangerous to contact Mary Grace directly, so I had a friend of mine slip a note inside her tote bag. Before they were onto me at CIA headquarters, I spent some time tracking your past and came across a corporation named

RBTL—the company that owns your mountain." Bobby grinned. "Sneaky name. Read Between The Lines is a computer acronym."

He turned serious once again. "At the same time, I got a list of your relatives, and that's how I knew about Fran. I was afraid they would go after Mary Grace because she's my sister and a reporter, and after reading your file, I knew Mary Grace would be safe with you. I went to the swamp shack in Georgia to leave two letters. One hidden for Mary Grace, the other in case you were with her. I knew you didn't trust me and wouldn't pay attention to the name I left you if you saw Finn on there. You worked together, and I figured you were probably friends, so I left that information for Mary Grace's eyes only, to do with as she felt best in case something happened to me. I knew if I went missing, she would eventually look there. Then I headed to Jackson Hole hoping to connect with both of you so that the letters at the swamp shack would never be needed."

A blush stole up his neck when he glanced at Fran. "I was hiking up the mountain, about to turn back around, because after thinking about it, I was afraid you might think I had something to do with the mission gone wrong, and that's when I heard a snowmobile. It turned out to be Fran."

"After we talked a little bit, I explained things to her, and at that point I needed some help. I had to trust someone. Fran agreed to hide me in a utility building behind the family home where she and her mother were staying. We both agreed for her to go to your cabin and see if Mary Grace was there, and maybe talk to you, see if she could find out if you blamed me for what happened.

But when she came back and told me about the explosion, and that you two were okay, I decided to stay put until I could come up with a plan."

He gazed at Mary Grace earnestly and her heart tripped with love. "I knew you'd be safe with Ned." He turned back to Ned. "I didn't find out anything new and figured you'd head to Washington. That's when Fran told me you had a town house here. We were hoping you would end up here. Fran had access to the security code and we waited inside, then came out here when we heard the garage door open."

Bobby shot Ned a nervous look and Mary Grace intervened before Ned had a chance to strangle Bobby for placing his niece in danger.

"Ned and I have a plan." She explained what they were planning to do, then said, "It's time for me to set up some interviews and plant some seeds." Mary Grace prayed Ned would forgive her when her real plan was revealed. One particular interview would be used as a tool to reveal the person she was sure was in this thing up to their neck.

NINETEEN

That evening, after having a pizza delivered, Ned made sure Fran and Mary Grace were ensconced in the two bedrooms. He left Mary Grace working away on a laptop he kept at the town house, and after tossing a few blankets around, he and Bobby shared the living room floor. He took immense satisfaction in the fact that Bobby tossed and turned all night long—hopefully out of fear. Ned made it clear he didn't trust Bobby, with his life or with his niece. Mary Grace's brother was going to have to prove himself to Ned.

Early the next morning, Mary Grace had insisted Ned call CIA Director Madeline Cooper because she'd promised her she'd run any kind of future story by the director first, due to possible security issues. She insisted the director would be aware of her movements due to her interest in what was going on.

Leaving the dogs with Fran and Bobby, they'd met at an out-of-the-way café and Ned was surprised at Madeline's response to Mary Grace's information implicating Chief of Staff Hensley in the involvement of selling state secrets. She'd been pleased. Maybe a little too pleased? Ned felt his soon-to-be ex-boss had jumped the gun when they found out later she'd gone behind Mary Grace's back and called a press conference for that day, which was where they were now. Leaning against a wall at the back of the room, Ned watched Mary Grace in her element. She was in the front row and the reporters surrounding her began shouting questions when the CIA director took the stage. She majestically held up a hand until the reporters quieted. Uneasiness rippled down his spine when Madeline Cooper looked at the group before she ducked her chin and hid a small self-satisfied smile. He straightened from the wall, his gut screaming and his eyes locked on the woman.

He glanced at Mary Grace and his unease strengthened in force. He recognized the determined jut of her chin. Something big was about to happen. Something he wasn't going to like and wasn't privy to.

The small smile was replaced by a forlorn expression as Madeline Cooper lifted her head and started talking. "Some unfortunate information has come to my attention. It will, of course, be investigated thoroughly, but I feel the American people have a right to know what's going on." She gripped both sides of the podium and leaned slightly forward. She had the reporters in the palm of her hand, everyone except Mary Grace.

"For some time now, we've been aware that state secrets have been making their way into enemy hands. There was one mission in particular that went awry because someone knew we were coming. I won't get into the details of that mission, but one of our people was severely injured during the process." She paused, then added dramatically, "They were betrayed and now we have information that sheds light on that unfortunate circumstance." She took a deep breath, drawing it out, gaining more time in the spotlight.

"We will be opening an investigation into Chief of Staff Hensley."

The room exploded, but Ned kept his gaze zeroed in on Mary Grace. The truth hit him like a fist in the chest and he knew what was coming. She had set up Madeline Cooper, actually wanting this press conference to happen. Betrayal sliced through him like a serrated knife. He watched and waited for the proverbial ax to fall.

Madeline Cooper held up a hand and the room quieted. Mary Grace shouted out a question before anyone could stop her.

"Director Cooper, isn't it true you were in a position to know the circumstances of the mission you just spoke about? Couldn't you have been involved in the selling of state secrets and a failed mission that left one of our own disabled for life?"

The director's head snapped up and her bewildered expression quickly turned to granite. "Just what are you implying, Miss Ramsey?" she asked stiffly.

Pushing aside the pain of yet another betrayal, Ned prepared to swiftly remove Mary Grace from the premises if things went bad.

"I'm implying that I've studied this situation from all the angles and I think you should be investigated instead of Chief of Staff Hensley." Mary Grace took a deep breath and plowed forward, using the CIA director's own words against her. "It has come to my attention that there's an offshore account in your name that shows recent activity. Did you, or did you not, transfer half a million dollars to someone right before, and right after, the mission that went wrong?"

Ned wanted to howl. Mary Grace had once again withheld information from him, and at the same time he was stunned that a woman he'd worked with for several years had fooled him.

Shock, and a touch of fear, shone in Madeline Cooper's eyes, but she closed the press conference with a bright, false smile. "I don't know where Miss Ramsey acquired her information, but I suggest her employer, Future Broadcasting Company, review her journalistic practices."

She turned to leave the podium and Ned pushed his way through the maddening throng of shouting journalists. He grabbed Mary Grace by the arm and shielded her as he bulldozed them through the crowd and out of the room.

She twisted around, facing him the moment they were clear, true regret written on her face. "Ned, I'm sorry I didn't tell you about Madeline Cooper, but you were so upset over Finn when I told you about him, I was afraid you'd try to stop me. After we met with Hensley, I got suspicious because I felt like he was innocent. Last night, I contacted the PI I hired earlier and had him dig deeper. Madeline Cooper tried to make it appear as if Hensley paid out the money, but my PI finally traced it all the way back to Madeline. She did a good job of covering her tracks, but not good enough."

Reporters were filing out of the room and several veered toward Mary Grace. He took her by the arm and started moving. "Let's get out of here. I want to speak to Madeline in private. I know where she lives. I've visited her house on two occasions over the past few years. I'd rather go alone, but I know you'll have none of that and I don't have time to argue."

He shoved his emotions into a box, closed the lid and didn't say another word until they pulled up to a gate protecting the privacy of the owner of a large house sitting at the end of a curved driveway. With gratification, he punched numbers into the box attached to a pole several feet from the gate.

Madeline hadn't had time to change the code. He stopped at the front entrance of the house and got out of the car. He was so angry that he didn't even notice Mary Grace had followed him until she laid a hand on his back. He heard a small sniffle and then, "I'm so, so sorry, but I didn't have a choice. I had to do this."

He ignored the warmth from her hand and stabbed the doorbell. The door swung wide and there stood the director's bodyguard.

Ned's fists clinched and he snarled. "I'm here to see her."

The bodyguard, Henry, recognized him and slapped out a palm. "You know the drill."

Ned handed over his cell phone and weapon and motioned for Mary Grace to hand over her own phone. Once they were over the threshold, Henry ran a wand over their bodies and winked.

"Wouldn't want any recording devices in the house. She'll see you in the library."

Ned strode forward and Mary Grace scuttled behind him. The library doors were open and he stepped inside. Madeline sat behind her antique cherry desk and motioned toward the two chairs across from her.

Ned strode up to the desk, leaned over and gripped the edge of the wood. "Tell me Mary Grace is wrong. Tell me you're not responsible for Finn ending up in a wheelchair. Tell me you haven't betrayed your country."

She tsked. "Now, Ned, I'm not happy that you and your little friend here have upset my plans for Hensley, but you know I won't go down for this. I have too much power."

Ned would make sure she was convicted for what she'd done, but he reined in his temper because, more than anything, he wanted answers.

"At least tell me this. I was working for you. Why were you trying to kill me and Mary Grace, and why did you transfer money into an offshore account in Finn's name? Was he a backup fall guy in case Hensley didn't work out?"

A sly grin filled with hidden secrets tilted her lips. She leaned forward and whispered, "I highly suggest you talk to your friend before you start accusing anyone of attempted murder."

Ned reared back as if she'd punched him. What was she implying? That she'd harm Finn if Ned came after her?

He had to ask. "What do you mean?" His words came out sounding hoarse.

She waved a hand at Henry, whom Ned had known all along was standing just inside the doorway.

"Henry, please show our guests out."

Ned shoved away from the desk and grabbed his weapon along with his and Mary Grace's phones from Henry's hand before he strode down the hall and out of the house. He wanted to hit something because he was afraid Madeline Cooper was going to hold Finn's innocence as collateral for her career. There was a trail of money movement, but that could disappear. She had the connections to make it happen.

He and Mary Grace got in the car at the same time and he tore out of there, slowing to a normal speed when they hit the street. He started to head back to the town house, but had himself together enough to spot the dark sedan coming up fast behind them. "Hold tight," he warned, just before he jerked the car down a residential side street, trying to rid them of their tail.

Mary Grace braced herself as the car took a sharp right. "Ned, what is it?" she asked tightly while trying to hang on. He took another hard left and her body swung in that direction.

"Looks like Madeline was one step ahead of us and had someone waiting until we left to tie up a loose end. The loose end being us. I should have paid better attention and we never should have gone there. It was a decision based solely on emotion and I know better." His voice sounded so cynical that Mary Grace didn't think anyone would ever be able to penetrate the wall of distrust that now surrounded him.

A bullet pinged the lower back of the car and Ned yelled, "Get down!"

Her heart hammering in her chest, she ducked and the car made several more sharp turns. She was about to sit up straight when the back of their car was rammed by the one chasing them. Her head hit the dash and stunned her for a second, but she rallied and looked sideways at Ned from her bent over position.

"Give me your gun," she said through gritted teeth. She'd had about enough of this whole mess and she was sick of getting shot at.

The look of surprise on his face was only momentary before he handed her his pistol. "You sure you know what you're doing?"

She glared at him before sitting up, opening her window and shooting at the car behind them. The first two bullets missed, but the third was a bull's-eye. She hit the right front tire and the vehicle swerved in the road until it finally hit a telephone pole.

She calmly handed the gun back to Ned and sat straight, staring out the window. She was tired of people trying to kill them, and if Ned wanted to crawl back to his mountain and hide, well, she'd deal with those emotions later. All she wanted right now was to hug Tinker Bell and have a few calm minutes to herself, but she did realize she needed to apologize, even if to deaf ears.

"Listen, I'm sorry about what happened. I know you trusted Madeline Cooper, but even if you never speak to me again, I had to handle things the way I did. If you had confronted her directly, which you would have, the truth would never have come out."

Having said that, Mary Grace also knew she wouldn't have changed the way she handled the situation. She was a seeker of truth, from a personal and professional standpoint. She prayed that Ned would understand, but his tight grip on the steering wheel indicated otherwise.

She was surprised when he finally spoke. "I'm fine with the way you handled the director, but I have one question."

"Yes?"

"Do you still think Finn betrayed me? That he was in league with Madeline Cooper?" He glanced at her bleakly. "Because if he is, that would mean my best friend has been trying to kill both of us." He gritted his teeth and his jaw worked itself back and forth. "For money."

Mary Grace wanted to tell him everything would be okay, but that wouldn't be the truth. As a child, she'd learned to face truth head-on, even if it hurt. Her mother and stepfather had forced her to learn that friends and family didn't always have your best interest at heart. She could literally feel his pain coming in waves, filling the car, and had no words to comfort him because deep inside she knew Finn had indeed betrayed his best friend, so she didn't say anything.

The car was quiet and they were soon back at the town house. Bobby and Fran were full of questions after seeing the press conference on television, but Mary Grace steered them away from Ned and into the kitchen. Ned disappeared into one of the bedrooms and closed the door.

She took a deep breath, pasted on a bright smile and faced her brother and Fran. "I think Ned needs some time alone. Why don't I make us some coffee?"

She scooped Tinker Bell into her arms when her precious baby came running into the kitchen full tilt, Krieger close on her heels. Burying her face in her dog's soft fur, Mary Grace felt the first tear fall for everything that could never be.

She felt a pair of thin arms wrap around her and Tinker Bell. Bobby gave her a good hug, then stepped back and pulled her toward a chair at the breakfast nook, gently pushing her into the seat.

"Come on, sis. You've looked out for me all my life. It's my turn to take care of you."

Mary Grace sniffed and lifted her head, staring at her brother with new eyes. "You grew up when I wasn't looking."

He glanced at Fran and blushed. "Yes, well, things change." He gave her a knowing, gentle smile. "You're in love with him, aren't you?"

Astounded, Mary Grace stared at the two of them as Fran sat down. The question didn't exactly catch her off guard, but…somewhere along the way, had she fallen in love with the gruff mountain man? A man who at times isolated himself on that mountain of his away from the world. A man filled with pain at the betrayals he had experienced. She looked deep within herself, and realized that yes, she had fallen in love with Ned. But it was an impossible situation, especially after this latest betrayal he'd experienced at the hands of Madeline Cooper. Mary Grace didn't think Ned would ever fully trust anyone again, especially her because she'd withheld information from him yet again.

Bobby arched a brow and Mary Grace responded, "Maybe, but nothing will come of it."

Bobby reached for Fran's hand. "Remember what Gram always says, 'Have faith. God can do anything. Even open the heart of a stubborn man.'" He paused and leaned back in his chair, changing the subject. "Tell us what happened today."

Placing Tinker Bell in her lap, Mary Grace shared everything that had happened, including her withholding information from Ned and someone shooting at and ramming their car. They were shocked at the audacity of the director of the CIA.

At the end of her tale, Bobby wrapped her hand in both of his on top of the table. "Listen, sis, if Ned really loves you, he'll come around. If he's foolish enough to allow other people's choices to stand in the way of love, then he's the one who will be left out in the cold."

Mary Grace closed her eyes and prayed they'd all live long enough to find out if Ned really could learn to trust and love someone.

TWENTY

The next morning, Ned announced they were flying to Scotland, and when they arrived at the tarmac, Madeline Cooper's sly innuendos about Finn still rang in his head, making him more determined than ever to prove his best friend's innocence. His patience wore thin when Bobby and Fran accompanied them to the airport, only to insist on boarding the plane when they arrived. They promised to stay out of the way and babysit the dogs when he talked to Finn.

He finally gave in just so they could be on their way. Without inviting Mary Grace to join him, he climbed into the cockpit and revved the plane's big engine. He'd filed a flight plan the night before, so if anyone checked, primarily the CIA director, they would know where he was headed. He'd be ready for them this time.

He concentrated on getting them off the ground, and soon they were soaring through the sky. It was going to be a long flight.

He brooded for the first four hours and no one bothered him, but soon after that, Mary Grace poked her head through the door with a cup of coffee and a Danish in hand. He thanked her curtly and she ducked back out.

He promised himself that after he proved Finn's innocence, he would get on with his life, but it was hard to think of the future when someone was trying to kill them.

He spent the rest of the flight planning what he would say to Finn and worrying about everyone's safety. Confronting Madeline Cooper had given them some answers, but if she was the one trying to kill them, he'd awakened the sleeping giant. They had given her one more reason to get rid of them all, including Finn.

He checked his watch after he set the plane down. It was 20:00 hours eastern time, which meant by the time they drove to where he'd stashed Finn it would be about two in the morning in Scotland.

He debated whether to wait but wanted to get it over with. He also considered whether to call Finn and warn him they were coming but decided against it. He trusted Finn, but his gut told him to make it a surprise visit so he could gauge his friend's reaction. That would help prove Finn's innocence to Mary Grace.

He left the cockpit and herded everyone off the plane. He waved at the guy who had stepped out of the building of the small airport and caught Mary Grace's small smile at the fact that he didn't have to handle any paperwork. That was going to change soon because he would no longer be working for the CIA.

He tried to prevent Bobby and Fran from getting into the car with him and Mary Grace, but Bobby insisted he was part of this and had a right to be there. Ned agreed with him, but they had a heated discussion when Fran refused to be left behind. Even the dogs hopped into the car.

Everyone was quiet while Ned steered the vehicle through the crystal clear night on small curvy country roads. The closer they got to the cottage where he'd stashed Finn, the more uneasy he became. He believed in his friend's innocence, but what if he were wrong? He was risking the life of everyone in the car.

He pulled to the side of the road a quarter of a mile from their destination and cut the engine. Mary Grace reached across the console and laid her hand on his.

"Ned, are you okay? We're in this together." She went quiet for a moment, then spoke in a soft voice. "For your sake, I pray Finn is innocent. I know how much his friendship means to you. But if he isn't, I pray God will give you the strength to overcome this."

A tumult of emotions clashed and roared inside him. He had always been a man of absolute control. His life had depended on it. He wanted to give something back to Mary Grace, but he was frozen inside. He found himself at a crossroads in life. If Finn were guilty, he didn't know if he'd ever be able to trust anyone again.

Slowly, he pulled his hand away and Mary Grace's warmth left him. He glanced into the back seat. "You two get out here." He pointed to the side of the road. "You can wait in that old shack."

They both opened their mouths to protest, but he placed a hand in the air. "This is not up for negotiation. Get out of the car. We'll pick you up on our way back."

They must have realized he meant business because they opened their doors and clamored out. Mary Grace rolled down her window and handed Tinker Bell to Fran. With a wobbly voice, she made Fran promise to take care of her beloved dog if something happened to her.

Ned wanted to howl in frustration. Nothing was going to happen to her because Finn was innocent. He just didn't want Fran and Bobby there to cloud the meeting. They'd pick them back up in an hour or so and everything would be fine.

Krieger had gotten out of the car and Ned cracked his window and gave a command. "Follow."

Mary Grace folded her arms over her stomach and stared out the passenger window at the thick forest and inky black night. "If you think Finn is innocent, why'd you leave them behind and order Krieger to follow on foot?"

Ned wasn't in the mood for chatter, but he answered curtly, "I didn't think it fair to Finn to involve anyone else in this discussion and it's force of habit with Krieger. He's always been my front man. He'll stay in the shadows until I tell him otherwise."

Ned knew Finn would be alerted by the security he himself had installed for his friend's safety. Finn would have a small warning that company was arriving, he just wouldn't know the identity of his visitors.

Ned's stomach churned the closer they got to the cottage, and all too soon, he pulled the vehicle into the short graveled driveway. Lights in the house were blinking on, and soon Mary Grace would know the truth, that Finn was innocent. Dressed in pajamas, Finn rolled his wheelchair onto the front porch, and in that moment, something that had been eluding Ned ever since the conversation he and Finn had had while Ned and Mary Grace were in Georgia crystallized in his mind, but it was too late. Too late for everything. Mary Grace had already slipped out of the car.

Exhaustion weighed heavily, but Mary Grace opened her car door when they arrived at Finn's cottage. She took a deep breath and said a quick prayer, because whatever happened would most likely determine the rest of her life. She had only known Ned a short time, but after talking to Bobby, she finally admitted to herself that Ned was the only man she'd ever love. The feelings she'd had for other guys she'd dated in the past didn't even come close to what she felt for Ned. She now realized it wasn't her dysfunctional childhood that had destroyed all her relationships. She just hadn't met the right man and her heart had known the difference.

She took a deep breath and studied the guy sitting in a wheelchair under the front porch light. He was light where Ned was dark. From a short distance, he appeared to be a good-looking man with blond hair and quite a good physique, considering he was confined to a wheelchair. He spotted Ned and waved them forward just as a large man stepped out of the house and stood at Finn's side.

Mary Grace kept moving but stopped when Ned met her at the front of the car. She saw him make a small movement with his right hand and surmised he knew where Krieger was and had just given him a command. That meant something wasn't right.

With a hand on her elbow, he moved them forward but spoke under his breath. "Be ready to move fast if I tell you to."

Questions burst forth in her mind, but she did as she

was told and walked to the front porch with a smile pasted on her face. "You must be Finn. I'm Mary Grace and I've heard so much about you." Her words didn't come out as smooth as she'd hoped, and Ned appeared relaxed at her side, but she knew he was wound tight. Tension radiated off him in waves. She didn't know what was going on, but his grip tightened on her elbow when his gaze swung from the large man standing at Finn's side to his friend.

"Why, Finn?"

Mary Grace's heart broke at Ned's pain-filled, gruff words.

Finn gave Ned a crooked grin. "You always were too smart for your own good. What gave me away?"

The man standing beside Finn pulled out a handgun and pointed it at them. Ned dropped his hand from her elbow in a seemingly natural manner.

"You did. When I spoke to you on the phone, you knew Mary Grace's name. I hadn't told you her name." He glanced at the big man standing beside Finn under the bright porch light. "Violet eyes. I saw your hench-man's unusual eye color when he tried to take down Mary Grace on my mountain. Did you have other hired men trying to kill us while your killer made his way back here? Were you behind all the attempts on our lives? Why, Finn? I thought we were friends."

Mary Grace readied herself to move when Finn's lips twisted into an ugly smile. "You have it all, Ned. You've always had it all." Eyes bright with jealousy and bitterness swung toward Mary Grace.

"Did you know Ned's a famous painter? He's known all over the world as the elusive *Ned* because the public has never met him. His family is rich, but he got even richer with his own paintings and he didn't even need the money. Did you know his family owns a huge castle here in Scotland?"

Finn glanced back at Ned. "I always tagged along during holidays—the charity case—and I promised myself one day I'd be as rich as your family."

Ned took a halting step forward and Mary Grace wanted to weep at the pain vibrating in his voice. "Finn, it doesn't have to be this way. We can work things out. I'll hire you the best attorney money can buy."

Finn shook his head and his lips twisted in a parody of a smile. "I really didn't want you dead, but I knew you'd never give up until you found out who had betrayed us. An admirable trait most of the time, but it was interfering with my plans. When Madeline Cooper and I realized Bobby had left one of the cameras running while our mission was being carried out, we knew we had to cover our tracks and dispose of anyone who might discover us. We figured Bobby would contact his sister, and if he actually knew anything he would share it with her, a well-known reporter. Oh, and we knew you were holed up on your mountain, we were just biding our time, hoping to make your death look like an accident, but then my man followed Mary Grace to your mountain and we had to try to get rid of both of you. I truly am sorry it has to end this way, but that's life. Oh, and one more thing before we say goodbye forever."

Mary Grace gasped when Finn pushed himself out of the wheelchair. Ned didn't move a muscle, just choked out one word. "Why?"

Finn's lips spread in a wide smile. "The bullet did graze my spine, but after I left the hospital and you moved me here, I hired a really good physical therapist. It was hard, but I regained my mobility." His lips twisted again. "The stupid guy who accidentally shot me is no longer with us." He shook his head in mock sorrow. "You just can't find good help these days."

"But why didn't you tell me you could walk?"

The grief and sadness in Ned's response made Mary Grace want to throw her arms around him and let him know everything would be okay, but that wouldn't be right because she didn't know if anything would ever be okay for Ned after a betrayal that cut this deep.

"Why, Ned, you wouldn't believe how many people underestimate a man sitting in a wheelchair. You're a prime example."

Finn glanced over his shoulder at his henchman and nodded. "Make it quick."

Everything happened at once. Ned shouted a German command for his dog, pulled a handgun from the inside of his jacket and pushed Mary Grace to the side in one smooth movement.

She went down sideways and her shoulder hit the graveled driveway, but she ignored the pain and scrambled to her feet. In a flash she saw Krieger coming up behind the big man holding the gun, but she knew it would be too late if the guy fired. She automatically threw herself in front of Ned just as both men's guns went off. She watched the large man fall as a burning sensation ripped through her side before she crumbled to the ground. She heard the loud report of a second shot, and from her prone position on the ground, prayed as she watched Ned move around her and charge his best friend. They struggled over a gun in Finn's hand. Krieger stood guard over the fallen body of the first man, saliva dripping out of his mouth.

Black dots peppered her vision, but she fought to stay conscious. She prayed nothing would happen to either man, because if Ned had to kill Finn in order to stop him, he would never forgive himself.

Just as her vision wavered even more, Fran slipped an arm under her head. She and Bobby must have followed them on foot, and Mary Grace was thankful they did. Fran's voice quaked as she spoke to Mary Grace.

"You have to be okay, Mary Grace. My uncle loves you and he'll never leave his mountain if you die."

Mary Grace wanted to reassure her, but the black dots were becoming thicker. Her heart jerked in fear when she saw Bobby out of the corner of her eye jump onto the front porch to help Ned, but Fran breathed out in satisfaction.

"It's okay. They have both men subdued and they're tying them up."

A few moments later, Ned bounded off the porch and kneeled at Mary Grace's side. He replaced Fran's arm with his own and leaned close, his heart pounding in fear that she'd been shot. Golden eyes filled with sadness and an expression he hoped was love stared back at him. It was in that moment he knew that all the betrayals in the world didn't matter as long as Mary Grace always looked at him as she was now. His heart expanded and filled with love for this feisty, beautiful woman, All the negative emotions he'd been clinging to—distrust, anger and betrayal—simply disappeared.

His Scottish brogue filled with gruff emotion, he said, "Aye, me luv, 'tis my fault this happened to ye. Ye have to hang on, ye hear me. I luv ye and find I canna live without ye." He pressed a gentle kiss against her forehead. A tear fell from his chin and hit her cheek before he whispered, "Ye saved me life, Mary Grace. I trust ye and I find meself trusting our Lord. I pray ye will live through this so I can shower ye wi' love for the rest of me life. Please say ye will marry me?"

Mary Grace's pain filled eyes stayed on Ned and the corners of her lips curved upward. "I love you back, Mountain Man, and yes, I'll marry you."

He bent down and gave her a warm kiss, then pulled back. "'Tis a happy man, I am, but if ye'd see fit to marry yerself to this mountain man this Christmas, I'd be the happiest fella on earth."

"I'll marry you, Mountain Man, if you'll rebuild that mountain cabin of yours." She gave him a shy grin. "I'd love to show our children where we first met."

A big whoop, something that sounded like a war cry from times past, filled the air and Ned kissed her again, right on the lips.

EPILOGUE

It was good that the bullet wound had just been a graze, because in her wildest imagination, Mary Grace never dreamed she'd be walking down the aisle of a five-hundred-year-old church on the grounds of an ancient castle on Christmas Day. Happiness surged through her as she stood at the entrance of the building, waiting for the "Wedding March" music to begin, and she said a silent prayer of thanks. The stone structure was bursting with people and the decorations were beyond beautiful. Simple but elegant small tree branches were attached to each pew with red bows and a huge Christmas tree stood behind the minister. The handmade ornaments on the tree looked as old as the church.

Her gaze found Gram Ramsey sitting proudly in the front row. Mary Grace's heart swelled at the thought of Ned flying her grandmother to Scotland and formally asking for Mary Grace's hand in marriage. He made a pledge to Gram that her home in Georgia would be in good hands for future generations. She chuckled, remembering Gram's response to *Eli*. "You'll do fine, my boy, just keep to the Word and everything will work out."

Bobby and Fran sat beside Gram, holding hands.

Mary Grace smiled, recalling the stir they'd caused by breaking tradition. Fran had insisted on sitting on the bride's side of the church with Bobby. That had brought quite a few raised eyebrows.

Her gaze swung to Laird Duncan, Ned's irascible grandfather sitting on the opposite aisle with Ned's gorgeous sister. Gram and Angus Duncan had enjoyed a few heated debates over the wedding, especially the short amount of time they had to plan it, but unless Mary Grace was mistaken, those two were keen on each other, as the laird's wife had died many years ago.

At last, she allowed her gaze to drift to the front of the church where Ned stood beside his older brother, both men standing tall and proud, dressed in historically befitting kilts. The clan's tartan colors were red and gray, and the church was filled with neighbors and friends wearing the same color. Early that morning, she had been presented with her own tartan sash, which she'd slipped over her white wedding gown.

The only kink in the day sat on the third pew, glaring at Ned's brother. The woman was an American librarian hired by Ewan to catalog the massive number of books in the old castle. Ned didn't trust the woman, said he sensed something off there, but Mary Grace ignored the moment of worry and turned her head to gaze at her future husband.

His smile rivaled the sun pouring through the church windows. He had come so far in such a short amount of time. He trusted her and had fully opened his heart to love. Finn's betrayal had hurt, but he finally realized he couldn't shoulder the burdens of the world—that was God's job. But it hadn't stopped Ned from trying to help Finn. He had indeed hired the best attorney money could buy. The rest was in God's hands.

The day before, Mary Grace had submitted her article. They'd found enough proof in Finn's cottage to force the CIA director to come under investigation, and Mary Grace alluded that Chief of Staff Hensley was instrumental in making this happen.

The music swelled in the small church and everyone stood. Her eyes trained on Ned, Mary Grace followed the path of pink rose petals and stopped at his side. She grinned and he smiled back. Before they turned to the minister, Ned surprised Mary Grace by whistling and looking back down the aisle. The whole church tittered when Krieger and Tinker Bell, both dressed in doggy tartans, padded down the aisle and sat beside their owners.

In a long Georgian drawl, Mary Grace brought more laughter to the congregation when she said, "You ready to get hitched, Mountain Man?"

"Aye, that I am."

* * * * *

If you enjoyed Holiday Mountain Conspiracy, *pick up these other thrilling stories from Liz Shoaf:*

Betrayed Birthright
Identity: Classified

Available now from Love Inspired Suspense!

Find more great reads at www.LoveInspired.com

Dear Reader,

Ned, my mountain man, appeared in my first two Harlequin books and I received quite a few requests for his story, so here it is. He has an abundance of secrets and journalist Mary Grace Ramsey is the perfect woman to uncover them all. As in most of my books, this one has a Southern flavor and both characters have faithful furry companions with their own canine romance blossoming. I took extra time and care developing both these characters, so please let me know what you think of them.

You can reach me through my website: www.liz shoaf.com.

Happy reading!
Liz Shoaf